Dear Reader,

I should have known Melinda Oliver was trouble from the morning I woke up in that hotel room with her. Well, not exactly *with* her . . . she was in one bed and I was in another.

It was a simple mix-up. I'm still finding it hard to believe that ridiculous incident could cause me to end up married to the woman and acting as a father figure to her niece and nephew! And now I've had to relocate to Delaware. Although I must admit, the charm of small-town America is alive and well in this state. And the chilly breeze from the river does add a certain romantic quality to the evenings—a roaring fire is a perfect way to warm up an evening, especially with Melinda by my side.

Of course, there aren't too many men who get to play the role of the knight in shining armor helping a damsel in distress save two children from a wicked step-grandmother. I suppose I should be flattered. But I've never pictured myself as the domestic type.

Sincerely,

John Medwin

Delaware

ELIZABETH AUGUST

Author's Choice

Delaware

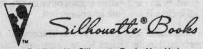

Silhouette® Books

Published by Silhouette Books New York

America's Publisher of Contemporary Romance

SILHOUETTE BOOKS
300 East 42nd St., New York, N.Y. 10017

AUTHOR'S CHOICE

Chapter One

It was almost exactly five weeks to the day since she had first met John Medwin when Melinda Oliver found herself driving through the rugged, north-central Pennsylvania countryside toward his home. The previous day's drive had been long, and around midnight she'd stopped, hoping to get some rest. This meeting wasn't going to be easy and she wanted to be fresh for it. But she hadn't slept well. In fact, she'd hardly slept at all. Every time she'd closed her eyes, she'd seen John standing on St. Louis Street in New Orleans watching her cab pull away with that look on his face that said "Good riddance!"

Finally she had given up the attempt to rest. Her stomach too knotted to eat, she'd resumed her drive as the sun barely began to peek over the Allegheny Mountains. The passing scenery was beautiful but she barely noticed. Like a recurring nightmare, those last thirty-six hours in New Orleans a month ago played over and over again in her mind.

They had begun so innocently. In her mind's eye she saw herself return to her hotel room, take a hot shower to relax her tired muscles and then call home.

"You and Joanie be good for Harriet and do what she says. *And*, stay out of the cookies until after lunch from now on," she admonished Frank, her seven-year-old nephew. He and his six-year-old sister had been her wards for the past two years, ever since their parents had died in a traffic accident. Her voice softening, she added, "I'll be home soon. I love you."

Hanging up the phone, she told herself for the umpteenth time that this separation was necessary. This was not a vacation. She was here on business. She had three mouths to feed, not to mention bodies to clothe and shelter.

She lay back on the bed with a groan. She was so exhausted the muscles in her face threatened to freeze in one position and remain fixed forever. Usually she liked meeting fans and booksellers—but at a slower pace than several hundred per day. Her publisher had insisted that attending this booksellers' convention would be a boon to her career. "You have a steady following and you sell reasonably well, but with this latest mystery we're aiming at the bestsellers' list," Lois Langley, her editor, had explained. "And the goodwill of the booksellers is important. How they promote your book in their stores can make a big difference in sales."

Melinda reached over to switch off the light, closed her eyes and was fast on her way to falling asleep when a knocking on the door pulled her back to consciousness. Maybe if I ignore it, whoever's there will go away, she thought hopefully, pulling the covers over her head.

The knocking became a pounding. "I know you're in there," a familiar male voice called from the other side. "Please, Melinda, this is important!"

For a long moment she lay perfectly still.

"Melinda, *please!*"

With a disgruntled moan she gave in to the inevitable and crawled out of bed. Pulling on her worn, but comfortable, floor-length terry-cloth robe, she belted it securely. Not bothering with her slippers, she ran her fingers through her short, thick black hair to smooth it into waves away from her face as she crossed the room and unlatched the chain. As soon as the door was opened, Gary Riley brushed past her and made a run for her television set.

"I taped an interview earlier today and it's going to air in five minutes," he explained, tuning in the local PBS station, then settling into a chair. Fiftyish and on the plump side, he was dressed in his usual three-piece suit and looked as if he'd already had a full night's sleep. "I made my strawberry tart and Gwyne's eggplant surprise. It's a shame she has the flu and couldn't come. I nearly ruined her recipe. Almost forgot the garlic."

Melinda liked the Rileys and counted them among her friends. The couple wrote cookbooks with clever anecdotes "sandwiched in," as Gwyne liked to say. They were easygoing people and normally she would have enjoyed Gary's company—but not tonight. "I'm happy for you," she said in apologetic tones, "but I'm just too tired to watch. If I don't get some sleep, I'm not even going to be able to spell my name tomorrow."

"These conventions can be tiring," he sympathized, remaining glued to his chair. "In fact, I accused Gwyne of faking the flu to avoid this rat race."

"Please, Gary, have a heart," Melinda pleaded, leaning against the wall to give her tired legs some relief. "Do you know why I'm standing? If I sit down, I won't be able to get back up. We younger people need our sleep."

"Tsk, tsk," he admonished playfully, then his expression became serious. "Would you believe that in this grand, plush hotel, my television set won't work? I called the desk, but they said they couldn't do anything about it until tomorrow."

"You're kidding." Inwardly Melinda groaned, hoping this whole situation was merely a bad dream from which she would wake at any moment.

"You really do look exhausted," Gary said. His face brightened. "Look, why don't you sleep in my room tonight?'

Too tired to argue and not wanting Gary to miss seeing himself on television, Melinda merely nodded in agreement. "I have to have my room back by seven tomorrow morning," she stipulated, throwing her toothbrush into her overnight bag.

"Seven," he promised.

Taking his key, she crossed the hall. Her room was a single with one double bed. The Rileys' room had been reserved by their publisher before they'd known Gwyne had to cancel, and it was a much larger room with two double beds. "At least he's orderly,'' Melinda muttered, passing the closet area where his suits hung neatly. She was in no mood to have to clear away jumbled clothing before lying down.

Dropping her overnight bag in a chair, she draped her robe over it, set her travel alarm on the bedside table and climbed into bed. For the brief second she was still conscious, she wondered if she had remembered to chain the door. But her body was too tired to care as she snuggled beneath the warm covers.

It seemed like only minutes later that the alarm began its insistent ringing. Covering her head with her pillow, she tried to ignore the sound.

''Shut that damn thing off!'' a groggy male voice demanded.

Melinda's eyes popped open. Throwing the pillow off, she turned over just as a firm male arm reached out from the second bed and slammed the travel alarm shut. Wiggling into a sitting position, she pulled the blanket up to her neck, gripping the edge of it so tightly her knuckles turned white.

"What? Who?" she demanded incoherently.

Groggy brown eyes focused on her. "Those are the same two questions I was about to ask you," her uninvited roommate growled.

Fear kept Melinda frozen momentarily as the man levered himself up on an elbow and stared across the small distance between the two beds. Like a trapped animal sizing up her foe, she focused on the interloper. His hair was thick and black. A full beard and mustache obscured his features—except for intense eyes so dark they almost matched his hair. He was at least six feet in length, and his exposed shoulders and partially exposed chest exhibited well-defined muscles. She knew that physically she would be no match for him. Her gaze shifted to the phone and, fighting down blind panic, she reached for it.

With an agility that startled her, he was out of his bed in an instant. His large bulk, clad only in a pair of briefs, loomed over her. As his hand closed over hers, preventing her from picking up the receiver, her control evaporated and unleashed fear took hold. She opened her mouth to scream, but before any sound could escape, he'd covered her mouth with his free hand. Frantically she began to struggle.

"Stop it!" he ordered, wincing as she bit into his palm. "I don't know who you are, but I, for one, don't want a scandal. Believe me lady, I have no intention of harming you. If you'll calm down and promise to behave, I'll let go."

The impatient anger in his voice was somehow reassuring; he wasn't any happier with the situation than she was. But Melinda wasn't ready to totally trust him. Her body still tensed to fight, she stopped struggling and nodded her agreement.

Cautiously, he released her. Then, still looming over her as if he didn't trust her to remain docile, he continued gruffly, "When I arrived yesterday, I discovered my room reservations had been screwed up and I didn't have a room for last night. Gary is an old friend. My agent mentioned Gwyne had come down with the flu at the last minute and hadn't come. He said Gary had a double room and suggested I ask if we could bunk together for one night. I managed to catch up with him just as he was leaving the hotel to do a television interview. He agreed to let me share his room for the night. Now what's your story?'' He paused, glaring down at her. ''And where's Gary?'' he added accusingly.

''He's in my room,'' Melinda answered tightly. Her fear had largely subsided, but in its place an unexpected internal struggle had developed that was making coherency difficult. She told herself she should be repulsed by the near nakedness of this strange man in front of her. Instead she was experiencing an odd curling sensation in her abdomen. ''His television wasn't working, so we exchanged rooms for the night.''

Raking a hand through his hair, the man moved back to his own bed and sank down onto it. A slight flush of embarrassment suddenly reddened his neck and he pulled his covers over his lower torso. ''Gwyne always said Gary was forgetful. But I never realized he could be *this* forgetful,'' he muttered angrily, adding a curse under his breath.

Melinda wasn't interested in discussing Gary's shortcomings. Moving to the far side of the bed, she tossed the covers aside and climbed out. She could feel the man's eyes almost like a physical touch as they traveled from her sleep-tousled hair downward to the T-shirt-style nightgown with Someone Loves You In Delaware inscribed across the front to the length of her exposed legs and bare feet. Unnerved by her acute awareness of his inspection, she grabbed her robe and, frantically pulling it on, fled to the door. Her roommate had chained it—something she promised herself she would never forget to do again no matter how tired she was. With shaking hands, she managed to unfasten it and escape into the hall.

A man lounged against the wall a couple of doors away. From his casual, touristlike clothing and the camera slung around his neck, she quickly surmised he was waiting for someone to accompany him on a tour of New Orleans. Normally she would have been embarrassed by a witness to her mad dash across the hall. But at this moment, she was glad not to be alone. Breathing a sigh of relief, she glanced over her shoulder to discover her uninvited roommate standing in the doorway of Gary's room. He'd hastily pulled on a pair of slacks and now leaned casually against the doorjamb watching her with a dry smile.

With what dignity she could muster, she knocked on the door of her room.

"Just like I promised," Gary said brightly as he opened the door, a wide grin on his face. "I'm dressed and ready to surrender your room back to you at the appointed hour. And if I do say so myself, I was magnificent." As he noticed the paleness of her complexion, his smile suddenly vanished. "You look as if you've seen a ghost."

"There's a man in your room," she replied in the same sort of voice one would use to tell a waiter there was a cockroach in the soup. "He says you invited him."

Glancing past her, Gary pressed his hand against his forehead. "John Medwin! Melinda, I'm so sorry! I completely forgot I'd told him he could share my room. That television interview really rattled me. I'm used to having Gwyne around to keep everything going smoothly. And, I will admit, I'm a bit forgetful. In fact, Gwyne says if my head wasn't attached to my body I'd walk off and leave it behind.''

"I may never speak to you again," she threatened, adding with a hiss, "I have never been so frightened."

"I'm truly sorry," Gary said, his face showing honest remorse. Turning his attention to the man across the hall, he said, "John, I'm ashamed of you. What in the world made you frighten a nice young woman like Melinda?"

"I've got to get dressed," Melinda snapped before John could answer. She had no desire to have a public discussion in the hotel hallway about what had just happened. Brushing past Gary, she entered her room and slammed the door behind her, chaining it securely. Then, standing with her back against the protecting barrier, she took a deep breath to calm her shaky nerves. *John Medwin*. As the name registered, she cringed. John Medwin, author of the Nicolus Blade spy novels where the women were gorgeous, with bodies that made men drool, clothed in silks and laces that left little to the imagination. According to rumor, John Medwin's real-life female companions, of which there were several, matched those in his books perfectly. Catching a glimpse of herself in the mirror, she had a tremendous urge to laugh. She must have been almost as much of a shock to him as he was to her. She was no raving beauty. She wasn't ugly; she just had a pleasant, sort of average face, and instead of being tall and model-slender, she was five foot four with an hourglass figure that threatened to drift toward pleasingly plump if she didn't fight her cravings for chocolate.

Her legs feeling sturdy once again, she moved away from the door. Tossing her robe on a chair, she looked down at her modest jersey nightshirt. A far cry from the peek-a-boo teddies Mr. John Medwin was used to, she thought dryly. The urge to laugh grew stronger. Then, realizing her reaction was probably due more to shock than amusement, she swallowed back the giggles. Tossing off her nightshirt, she went into the bathroom to shower.

She was drying her hair a few minutes later when a knock interrupted. "If it's Gary wanting to use my television set again," she muttered, making certain her robe was secure, "I have half a mind to throw it at him."

Leaving the chain in place, she opened the door to find John Medwin on the other side. A flush of embarrassment washed over her.

"I thought you might be needing this," he said with studied politeness, holding up her overnight bag.

"Yes, thank you," she managed coolly. He was fully dressed now, in slacks, a lightweight pullover and a sport coat, but in her mind's eye she still saw the expanse of bare chest and long muscular legs. With the image again came the warm curling in her abdomen. You're twenty-seven; stop acting like a teenager, she scolded herself curtly as she closed the door and unfastened the chain, then reopened the door.

"I wanted to apologize for this morning," he continued stiffly. "When I came into the room last night, I saw a sleeping body and assumed it was Gary. I didn't want to disturb him, so I very quietly went to bed. It was an honest mistake.''

She sensed anger behind his polite facade. He's probably afraid his reputation will be ruined if anyone finds out he shared a hotel room with someone as mundane as myself, she mused acidly. Pride glistened in her eyes. ''This morning was a shock and embarrassment to both of us. As far as I'm concerned, it's best forgotten.''

His jaw relaxed. ''Agreed,'' he said, and without another word, he picked up his suitcase and walked down the hall.

She stepped out into the hallway and turned to watch his retreating back. ''I'm the one who's supposed to be the angriest about an incident like this,'' she muttered as she saw him press the elevator button with a strong, furious jab. ''I'm the woman. I'm the one with the reputation to protect. Who does he think he is anyway?''

''It's not you personally,'' Gary's voice sounded in a whisper behind her. Down the hall, the elevator door opened and John Medwin stepped inside. Waving goodbye to the tall, bearded man, Gary called out cheerily, "See you later, John."

"Later," came the gruff reply as John's dark eyes traveled grimly over Melinda as if making one final inspection of the damage he might have done to his reputation.

"What an infuriating man! From the way he acted, you'd think I personally screwed up his reservations and wrecked your television set just so he and I would end up in the same room," she said through clenched teeth.

"He just doesn't trust women in general," Gary explained in pacifying tones. "I don't know the whole story. I do know that after his father died, his mother turned him over to an orphanage. I suppose she couldn't afford to raise him on her own. Whatever the reason, he told me once that as far as he's concerned, motherly love is a well-preserved lie and women are as fickle as the weather. Excepting Gwyne, of course."

Self-righteous indignation flamed in Melinda's eyes. "Just because he's spent his life being exposed to the wrong kind of woman doesn't give him the right to condemn all of us.''

Gary rewarded her observation with a smile and a friendly wink. ''I'll tell him you said that. Now I've got to run. Thanks for the use of your television last night.''

''Don't you dare tell John Medwin anything I said,'' she called after him. Then, realizing she was still in her robe and she was supposed to be meeting Ruth James, her agent, in less than half an hour, she slipped back into her room and began to dress hurriedly.

Standing in the entrance of the dining room a little while later, she scanned the tables for Ruth. A pair of giggles from a corner table caught her attention. Glancing in the direction of the sound, she found herself looking into John Medwin's shuttered brown eyes. The giggles were coming from the stunningly beautiful blonde and brunette seated at his table, obviously enjoying his company. Again a strong wave of inadequacy washed over her. Curtly she reminded herself that she could chew gum and walk at the same time—a feat she doubted either of those women could accomplish without help. Swinging her attention back toward the center of the room, she breathed a sigh of relief when Ruth suddenly stood and waved.

"I saw you glancing toward John Medwin," Ruth said as Melinda joined her. "I'd love to handle him, and I don't mean just as a client."

"I suppose if you like the cynical, macho type who's only interested in women for their bodies, he'd be perfect," Melinda returned dryly.

"I met him at a party once," Ruth continued, refusing to be put off by Melinda's cut. "He can be very charming."

"So can a king cobra," Melinda tossed back, trying to concentrate on her menu but finding the giggling coming from John Medwin's table exceptionally grating.

Reaching across the table, Ruth tilted Melinda's menu down so she could look her in the eye. "What happened between the two of you? Get into a fight over an elevator or a taxi?" she questioned with interest.

Melinda regarded her agent with schooled innocence. "What are you talking about?"

"I read people, that's part of the key to my success. I know you wouldn't take an instant dislike to someone for no reason, and John Medwin has glanced—how shall I put it?—" for a moment Ruth paused in thought, then said "—with a sort of guardedness, toward this table three times since you sat down."

"Have you ever considered writing romance novels?" Melinda questioned, determinedly raising her menu again.

"No. But I do enjoy reading them," Ruth admitted, studying Melinda even more closely. Then prudence evidently tempered her curiosity as she studiously turned her attention to her menu.

Nine hours later Melinda returned to her room and collapsed on her bed. She could swear she had met every bookseller twice during the past two days. Thank goodness it was almost over. She was tempted to skip the cocktail party her publisher was hosting that evening and sneak away to see New Orleans.

This evening would be her last possible chance to wander through the French Quarter. Tomorrow she'd be flying home. She knew the sudden loss of their parents had left deep scars in Frank and Joanie, and although they loved Harriet and didn't mind staying with her, Melinda was their source of security. This trip had kept her away for four days already, and she'd heard the underlying anxiety in their voices the night before when they'd asked when she would be coming home. Her concern for them would not allow her to take even one extra day for sightseeing.

And then there was Adelle. She could never be certain what plot the woman was cooking up to try to get custody of the children. Shaking off the chill caused by the thought of Frank and Joanie's step-grandmother, Melinda looked out her window. A jazz quartet dressed in bright costumes was slowly dancing its way up the street, and she felt the city beckoning.

"Business first!" she ordered herself firmly, promising herself one last trip down Bourbon Street before bed. Breathing a tired sigh, she showered and dressed for the cocktail party. Trying to look on the bright side, she reminded herself that Gary had the same publisher and therefore would be there. *And so will John Medwin,* a little voice within her interjected on a sour note.

"John Medwin—along with Miss Tweedledee and Tweedledum," she muttered. The man had spent a large portion of the day signing autographs at a table across the aisle from her, the two striking women acting as his gofers, getting him coffee and soft drinks, massaging his back, feeding his ego. She scowled at herself. Why should she care who John Medwin spent his time with?

"I don't care!" she informed the image in the mirror tersely. "I'm just sick and tired of all the giggling."

Giving her hair one final brush, she grabbed her purse and left her room.

Chapter Two

The air-conditioning was no match for the crowd at the cocktail party. Assailed by a wave of body-heated air and the sound of a hundred people all trying to talk at once, Melinda almost turned away at the door. But reminding herself this was business, she forced herself to go inside. Almost immediately she heard the familiar giggling. Glancing in the direction from which it came, she saw John Medwin and his two companions standing in the midst of a circle of admirers. The men, she noticed, were paying more at-

tention to the blonde and the brunette than
to the author. And well they might, she
thought. The dresses the women wore were
backless, and the necklines of both plunged
nearly to their waists. Glancing down at her
own conservative dress, it occurred to Melinda that it probably used more fabric than
their two dresses combined. For a moment
she felt spinsterish. Then, furious with herself for allowing the man and his female
companions to affect her so strongly, she
turned her attention to the rest of the people
in the room. She wasn't in the mood to make
conversation and wanted a place to blend
in unobtrusively. Spotting Gary, she attempted to melt into the group around him.
He was telling one of his many stories and
would easily be able to carry the conversation single-handedly.

But her ploy didn't work. Ruth found her.
"I've got some booksellers who are anxious
to meet you," the agent insisted and, taking
Melinda by the arm, guided her across the
room.

To Melinda's chagrin, they ended up near
John Medwin. It was the blonde who had

the most irritating giggle, she decided as she
made polite conversation with Ruth and the
booksellers. It sort of penetrated one's skull
like a high-pitched bell. Finally Melinda
could stand being in the room no longer.
Saying her goodbyes to the group, she
quickly made her escape.

A veranda at the rear of the hotel looked
out onto a small garden. Melinda had discovered this peaceful refuge the first morning of her stay in New Orleans, and it had
become one of her favorite spots. Without
even thinking about where she was going,
she wandered out onto it. To her relief, both
the veranda and the garden beyond were deserted.

Dusk was just beginning to settle, and the
sweet scent of flowers perfumed the air.
Leaning against one of the wooden pillars
supporting the protective roof, she stared out
at the fountain that was the centerpiece of
the small, walled garden. The evening was
hot and sultry, and her mind drifted into a
half-dream state. Once again she saw John
Medwin lying in the bed beside hers, raised
up on an elbow, studying her with those dark

eyes of his. Her hand trembled with the desire to reach out and touch him, to test the warmth and firmness of his flesh.

Tilting her head back so it, too, leaned against the sun-heated pillar, she closed her eyes. A burning knot formed in her abdomen as she wondered what it would have felt like to be kissed by him. The beard would probably scratch, she thought, curtly interrupting this line of thought. That she was having such a sensuous daydream—and about a man like John Medwin—shocked and appalled her. He was most certainly not her type. I've been a virgin too long. It's done something strange to my mind, she decided.

"Thought you might like a drink." The male voice broke into her solitude.

Startled, wondering if her imagination had taken total control of her mind, her eyes shot open to discover the object of her unwanted fantasy standing in front of her.

"Don't worry, I won't turn you in to the authorities," he said, extending a glass of white wine in her direction.

"Turn me in?" She frowned to cover the embarrassment his unexpected arrival sent washing over her. What would he think if he knew what had been on her mind?

"You look as guilty as a child caught playing hooky," he elaborated, picking up her hand and placing the wineglass in it.

His touch was warm, sending a tingle up her arm. It's just nerves and tiredness, she assured herself. Aloud, she said with cool control, "I needed some fresh air." Remembering her manners, she added, "Thank you for the drink."

"You're welcome," came his easy reply.

Looking up into his face, she saw the cynical humor in his eyes. "I'm sure you must be missed, inside," she said frostily.

He ignored the dismissal in her voice, and challenge mingled with the humor in his eyes. "Gary tells me it's your opinion I hang around with the wrong sort of woman."

"Gary has a way of twisting what people say." Turning her attention toward the fountain, she made a mental note never again to say anything personal in Gary's presence that she would be embarrassed to have repeated. "I have no interest in what women you spend your time with."

Catching her chin in his hand, he turned her face toward his. There was an intensity in the way he was studying her that made her legs feel suddenly weak. "It seems incongruous to have spent the night in the same bedroom with a woman I've never kissed. And I've been wondering all day what it would be like to kiss the 'right sort' of woman."

His face moved toward hers. She knew she should turn away, but the desire to satisfy her own curiosity was too strong to resist.

Setting his drink on the banister, he lifted his hand to her neck and began to gently massage the taut cords.

Every nerve in her body awoke as anticipation mingled with fear. Defensively, she set her drink aside and brought her hands up to press against his chest. But as her palms molded against the fabric of his shirt, she exerted no pressure. Instead the breath locked in her lungs as the solid feel of him burned its impression into her flesh. Frantically she tried to think of something flippant to say. But her mind was focused too intently on what was happening.

The brown of his eyes darkened with purpose.

His beard and mustache brushed against her skin as their lips met. She had expected to be repulsed by the feel of it, but instead waves of heated excitement shot through her.

The kiss, too, was not what she'd expected. It wasn't harsh and demanding, it was warm and inviting. He kept the contact light at first, teasing her lips with the heat of his mouth. When she offered no resistance, he deepened the kiss.

The blood ran hot through her veins. Feeling dizzy from the surge of heat he stirred within her, she curled her fingers around the fabric of his shirt for support.

Nibbling gently on her lips, he lightened the contact again, then broke it entirely. She almost groaned with disappointment as their mouths parted.

As if sensing her reluctance to have the kiss end, he kissed her again lightly. Then, keeping his face in close proximity to hers, he looked hard into her eyes. ''I have the impression you've never been properly kissed before.''

Melinda's back stiffened. He was making fun of her again. ''Of course I have,'' she said, ordering her fingers to unwrap themselves from his shirt. ''I've just never been kissed by a man with a beard before. It was ... interesting.''

''I'm willing to show you just how interesting I can be,'' he offered.

She swallowed hard. His thumb was massaging the hollow behind her ear, sending hot currents through her body. She hadn't felt an urge this strong since her first adolescent case of puppy love. She had fought her desire then, and sanity told her that unless she was interested in a one-night stand, she had better fight it now. ''No thanks,'' she said, this time putting force behind her hands to push him away.

Without a struggle, he released her and took a step back. The cynical amusement returned to his eyes. ''I suppose there's a nice little boyfriend back home to whom you've sworn total devotion?''

"Yes," she lied, then told herself it wasn't entirely a lie. She was devoted to Frank. The fact that he was her nephew and only seven years old was none of John Medwin's business.

He ran his thumb across her lips, still warm and soft from his kiss. "If I were him, I wouldn't let you out alone too often."

The implication that she would be easy prey for any man willing to make the effort had the effect of an icy shower. "He doesn't have to worry," she assured him frostily.

The contemptuous smile that spread over John's face called her a liar. "The passion I saw in your eyes was not my imagination. In fact, it was hot enough to make me momentarily reconsider the 'sort of woman' I usually keep company with. Thank you for reconfirming my assessment of the feminine sex—and restoring my faith in my choice of company."

"John." The blond beauty who'd been hanging on his arm all day came out onto the balcony. "Lanie and I have been looking all over for you." She stopped when she saw Melinda. The smile on her face remained on her mouth but left her eyes. "Sorry," she said. "I didn't mean to interrupt."

"You didn't," he assured her, taking a step toward her and wrapping an arm around her waist. "Miss Oliver and I were simply discussing various philosophies about relationships."

Ignoring Melinda, the blonde smiled brightly at John. "If you're finished, Lanie and I are ready to go paint the town like you promised."

"Let's start with Bourbon Street," he said, guiding her toward the lobby. "I feel like hearing some good hot jazz."

As they disappeared back into the hotel, John whispered something into his companion's ear. The woman's giggle floated back to Melinda and her stomach knotted. Frustration filling her, she swung her gaze back to the fountain. She wanted to be angry with John Medwin, but her real fury was directed at herself. She *had* been kissed before. How could she have been so weak as to practically melt into his arms? Ever since the children had become her responsibility, all of her spare time had been devoted to them.

Clearly, this had been a mistake. *As soon as I get home, I'm going to start dating seriously again,* she promised herself. *I must be starved for male companionship if a man like John Medwin can affect me so easily.*

"A bunch of us are on our way to Bourbon Street." Ruth's voice interrupted Melinda's self-berating. "Why don't you join us? That ominous expression is a sure sign you need company."

"No thanks, I really do have a headache." Melinda forced a smile as she turned to face her friend. She had no desire to accidentally run into John Medwin and his two leechlike companions again this evening. "And I have an early flight home tomorrow."

"Headache or not, New Orleans is not a city to miss a chance to see," Ruth persisted.

"I'm really not interested."

Concern replaced Ruth's encouraging smile. "You should have some fun. This instant parenthood business has made you much too serious." Then, seeing the determination in Melinda's eyes, she gave a small helpless shrug. "Take two aspirin, and I hope you feel better in the morning."

"Thanks." Melinda breathed a sigh of relief that Ruth wasn't the pushy type when it came to personal relationships. Going up to her room, she made her nightly call home to assure herself that Frank and Joanie were all right.

Hanging up a few minutes later, she walked over to the window and looked out at the street.

Rebellion suddenly filled her. Staying in her room just because she didn't want to run into John Medwin was ridiculous. She had promised herself one more excursion through the busy nightlife of the French Quarter. On top of that, a plot for a new murder had begun to form in her mind and it revolved around Bourbon Street. She needed to walk the area at night again, this time making more intensive mental notes and a few written ones. Grabbing a shawl, she flung it around her shoulders with a flourish and left her room.

Walking to Jackson Square, she purchased a bag of *beignets* and a cup of the customary, strong, chicory-flavored coffee. Munching on the fried donuts, she gazed out over the Mississippi River. This, she decided, was the perfect spot for her heroine to begin retracing the murder victim's steps. Taking out a notebook, she set her coffee and bag of *beignets* aside and jotted down a few descriptive notes about the traffic on the waterway.

Then, eating the last of the little fried rolls, she began her trek. She chose to leave the square by way of St. Ann Street because it added an extra block of Bourbon Street to her route. Following the narrow roadway, she entered Bourbon Street to find herself in the midst of what seemed like one gigantic party. Drinks were served in plastic glasses so patrons could wander freely and not be tied to one bar or night spot too long. Adding a raucous flavor, strip joints were intermingled with the jazz clubs. "A sleazy party at times," she jotted down as she paused at the entrance to one of the strip joints to view the photographs of the almost-nude dancers advertising what was in store for those who entered.

A jazz quartet was performing on a street corner, and Melinda stopped to listen to the music and jot down a quick description. Then, tossing a dollar into the open trumpet case in front of the group, she continued to weave her way through the groups of laughing partiers.

Suddenly a large hand closed around her arm. Startled, she turned to tell her captor he had better release her immediately. But the words froze in her throat as she again found herself looking up at John Medwin's heavily bearded features.

"Gary spotted you wandering alone and sent me to ask you to join us," he said coolly, releasing her as if he found touching her distasteful. With a nod of his head, he indicated a jazz club a few doors down. "He and the others have gone in to get a table."

It was obvious John didn't like the idea of asking her to join his group. Pride overcame prudence. "Taking Gary along on your sordid excursion in an attempt to corrupt his marriage?" she asked. "I'm surprised you're willing to share your female companions." Even before the last words were out, she wished she'd held her tongue as the cynical amusement once again shone in John's eyes.

"We are a large group, not a foursome. In fact, I believe your agent is also one of our number."

She'd made a fool of herself again! Why in the world had she brought up the subject of his female companions? Attempting to recover her dignity, she said with schooled politeness, "Tell Gary thank you for the invitation. But I prefer to go my own way." Putting action to her words, she resumed her trek down the street. Why hadn't she simply said that in the first place? she chided herself.

She'd gone about five paces when John's hand closed over her arm again. Jerking free, she glared up at him. "What do you want now?"

He scowled down at her impatiently. "Gary seems to think you're an innocent who needs watching over. Personally, I have my doubts about that. However, I don't think it's wise for a single woman to be wandering around down here alone at night. It's asking for trouble.''

She had to admit he might have a point, but he'd also delivered a sharp jab she couldn't ignore. This time, however, she was determined not to overreact. "You and I mix like oil and water, Mr. Medwin," she said coolly. "It would ruin both our evenings to spend time together, even in a large group. Therefore, I suggest you go back to your friends and leave me to my fate." Again she walked away from him. A prickling sensation on the back of her neck caused her to glance over her shoulder. He was standing where she'd left him, watching her. Abruptly, he turned in the direction from which he'd come and in long strides began to retrace his steps.

"Good riddance," she muttered aloud. Silently she assured herself that with the large crowd of people milling around on the street, she was perfectly safe.

Reaching the intersection of Bourbon and St. Louis streets, she turned right onto St. Louis. St. Louis, No. 1, the cemetery at the corner of St. Louis and Basin Street, was her destination. It was not only the oldest and most famous cemetery in New Orleans, but Marie Laveau, a very powerful voodoo queen, was buried there. It was, Melinda had decided, the perfect spot for her victim's body to be found.

It was also one block beyond the recognized boundaries of the French Quarter. The farther she moved away from Bourbon Street, the fewer people she saw. The homes and museums that were open to tourists during the day were now closed. A few blocks farther, she found herself completely alone.

The young woman moved slowly up the street with purpose, she composed mentally. *Footsteps sounded behind her.*

Footsteps! A cold chill ran down Melinda's spine. She actually did hear footsteps behind her. She looked ahead and to both sides. The streets were deserted except for whoever was behind her. She picked up her pace and the footsteps picked up theirs. Quickly she considered her options. She could try to outrun whoever was following her. She was almost to the cemetery—she could duck inside and hide behind one of the large beehive tombs. But there were a lot of stories connected with that cemetery; many people believed Marie Laveau's powers could reach beyond the grave. Just superstition, she assured herself. Still, she wasn't enthusiastic about testing it. There was something eerie about the place even in broad daylight.

Readying her legs to run, she glanced over her shoulder. A curse formed in her mind as her muscles tightened and she swung fully around. "You scared me half to death!" she addressed her pursuer accusingly.

John Medwin regarded her narrowly. "You could use a good scare to knock some sense into you! Don't you know that wandering around alone at night in a strange city is dangerous? I could have been a mugger, or worse. You aren't even in the French Quarter any longer!"

"I can take care of myself," she returned with a firmness she didn't feel.

"One thing I can't abide is a fool!" he growled, and turning abruptly away, he started back toward Bourbon Street.

"Me, neither!" she muttered angrily at herself as the sense of aloneness began to close in on her again. Jogging, she caught up with him. "You're right. It was stupid of me to come here alone," she said tersely, when he glanced over his shoulder at her. "It just galls me to admit it. We seem to have a way of rubbing each other the wrong way."

Slowing his pace so she could fall into step beside him, he said nothing.

His silence was worse than his jibes.

"Why did you follow me?" she asked, wondering why he would go to so much trouble for someone he obviously didn't like being around. "I thought you'd returned to your friends."

"I started to," he answered grimly. "But Gary asked me to make certain you were safe and I gave him my word I would. I glanced back and saw you turn onto St. Louis Street. I assumed you were going to find a taxi and return to your hotel, but a nagging little voice insisted I make certain. Gary would ask where you were, and I didn't want to tell him anything that might turn out to be less than the truth." Pausing, he glanced toward her. The look on his face suggested he thought her elevator didn't go all the way to the top floor. "I must admit it never occurred to me you would decide to take a stroll to the cemetery."

Pride demanded she defend her behavior. "I wanted to walk this route at night because I'm thinking of using it in a book."

The scowl on his face darkened. "You're lucky you're not tomorrow's headline: St. Louis, No. 1 Eerie Setting for Mystery Writer's Death."

She'd admitted she'd behaved without thinking. The least he could do was be gracious instead of continuing to rub salt in the wound. Clamping her mouth shut, Melinda walked beside him in stony silence.

They were almost back to Bourbon Street when she spotted a taxi letting passengers off. Picking up her pace, she hailed it. The very last thing in the world she wanted was to spend a second more in this man's company. "You can tell Gary I've gone back to my hotel," she said coolly as the taxi came to a halt beside her. Giving the driver her destination, she slipped into the back seat. As the taxi drove away, she glanced over her shoulder. John was standing where she'd left him, watching her departure. On his face was that grim look that seemed to question her sanity.

Chapter Three

Now it was her turn to question her sanity.
As her mind returned to the present, forcing
the New Orleans images to fade, she again
desperately searched for a way out of this
meeting. But there was none.

"You know how bullheaded Judge Craras
can be," she remembered Philip Ross, her
lawyer, saying in that fatherly voice of his.
"And he's a very conservative man. Even
though it was a provision in their wills, it
wasn't easy to convince him to allow you to
raise the children on your own following

your brother and sister-in-law's deaths. He didn't like the idea of Frank and Joanie being raised by a young, single woman. Adelle Upton had age and a standing in the higher social echelons of Wilmington society. She was able to put up a good fight for her grandchildren.''

''Step-grandchildren,'' Melinda had corrected.

''Precisely. Step-grandchildren,'' Philip had repeated her correction. ''The fact that the children are not her actual flesh and blood was probably the deciding factor at *that* time.''

Melinda knew that Philip's age—he was nearly sixty-seven—and his reputation for being an honest, conservative, thoughtful, caring man had also gone a long way toward swaying Judge Craras the first time. But this renewed attack by Adelle was different. This time she could win.

Ahead she saw the mailbox described in the quickly jotted directions to John Medwin's home, and her hands tightened on the wheel. ''Now I know what a true act of desperation is,'' she muttered. Turning onto the

long private drive, she was met by a wooden
gate barring her way. A large sign attached
to the gate announced that this was private
property and threatened trespassers with
prosecution.

"A welcome in keeping with our phone
conversation," Melinda mused, recalling
how cool he had been about granting her this
meeting. For the hundredth time, she was
tempted to turn back. But the fear of losing
Joanie and Frank was stronger than her fear
of being humiliated. Resolutely she climbed
out of her car and swung the gate open.

Driving through, she stopped on the other
side to close it. "You know this is a fool's
errand," she told herself as she climbed back
into her car and continued up the drive. *But
I have to try.*

Woods bordered the road for nearly half
a mile before they gave way to a large clearing. In the center of the clearing was an
A-frame house made of cedar. A mud-
splattered Jeep sat in the drive.

Her legs felt unsteady as she left her car
and walked toward the house. "This is
crazy," she told herself again. Vividly she

recalled the two leggy beauties who had clung to him during the convention. Pausing for a moment, she tried to gain strength from the quiet solitude of the surrounding woods, but her nerves were too taut. Again she was tempted to turn back. Again the images of her niece and nephew looking up at her trustingly stopped her. She had to at least try. Still, as she started up the steps to the door, every cell in her body rebelled.

Suddenly the door was opened and she found herself face-to-face with John Medwin. He was wearing faded jeans and an old sweatshirt with the sleeves and neck cut out. Obviously he considered the prospect of her visit so unimportant he'd made no attempt to dress for it.

"Are you coming in, or do you plan to stand on my porch and state your business?"

Realizing she had frozen in midstep, Melinda forced her legs to carry her forward, but as she reached the door, the desire to bolt was overwhelming. She stopped suddenly on the threshold.

An impatient frown etched itself into John's features. "You have nothing to fear from me. I don't bite, and my house is presentable."

"I'm not afraid of you or of facing a bachelor's unkempt home," she said levelly as she forced herself once again into motion and continued into the house.

Letting the screen door swing closed, he led the way into the large, cathedral-ceilinged living room. "Then what are you afraid of?"

In contrast to John Medwin, Melinda had dressed carefully for this meeting in a conservative, well-cut, pale gray business suit. She'd worn high heels to give her height. But the clothes weren't helping as he continued to regard her as if she was an unwanted intrusion.

"Humiliation." The thought was so strong in her mind, the word came out of its own accord.

The frown on his face deepened. "Humiliation?"

"I am afraid of humiliating myself," she elaborated honestly. There was interest behind the coldness in his eyes now. And soon there will be laughter, she mocked herself, again tempted to bolt. But her feet remained firmly planted. "My reason for coming here is not easy to explain," she continued stiffly, thinking it was the biggest understatement of her life. "I'm not exactly certain how to begin."

"Would you like to sit down?" he offered, his previous impatience replaced by guarded politeness.

She shook her head in the negative. "No. I think I can do this better standing up."

"Suit yourself." Lowering himself into an overstuffed armchair, he studied her narrowly.

Melinda paced the room. She had been over what she had to say to him a thousand times. There just wasn't an easy way. Coming to a halt behind the companion chair to the one he occupied, she stood with her hands resting on its back. "My brother and sister-in-law were killed in an automobile accident about two years ago. They left two children, Joanie—she's six—and Frank, who's seven." She saw him raise an eyebrow slightly. He probably hates children, she thought frantically. I knew this was a fool's errand. Again she was tempted to forget this whole business. Instead, she drew a deep breath and forced herself to go on.

"My parents are dead. My brother and his family were the only close relations I had. I spent a great deal of time with them, and I took care of Joanie and Frank whenever Judy and Kent wanted to get away for a while. Judy also had very little family. Her father died several years ago. She had an aunt, Aunt Mae, with whom she was close, but Aunt Mae is in a nursing home. Judy also had a stepmother, Adelle." The mention of Adelle's name caused Melinda's jaw to tighten.

"Adelle had no time for Judy or Judy's children when Judy was alive. In fact, from the moment Adelle married Judy's father she worked to alienate father and daughter. Judy's father was a reasonably wealthy man, and Adelle had no desire to share his money with anyone. She managed to create so strong a rift between Judy and her father that Judy finally moved out. When Judy and

Kent married, her father didn't even attend the ceremony. It was as if Judy was as much an orphan as Kent and I. It was only natural for the three of us—and the children, when they came along—to form a very close family unit. And it was reasonable that in their wills Judy and Kent named me as guardian of their children.

"Judy's father had died soon after Judy's wedding, leaving everything to Adelle. Judy did attend his funeral. Adelle completely ignored her. From the moment Judy left her father's house, Adelle never sought her out and didn't come to see the children when they were born or anytime afterward. So I was surprised when she came to Judy and Kent's funeral. I was even more surprised when she hugged the children and put on a tremendous show of being the concerned grandmother.

"Next she started spreading stories that made it look as if it had been Judy's immaturity that had caused the rift between Judy and her father. Adelle even claimed she had attempted to mend the breach. At first I was confused, then I realized she must have learned about the insurance." Melinda's hands tightened on the back of the chair.

"My brother was not a wealthy man, but he was a careful one and he took his responsibilities seriously. I suppose most people would think he was overinsured, but he was merely reacting to our own parents' deaths. They died when he was barely twenty-one and I was fifteen, and they left nothing. He was in his junior year of college, studying to be a doctor, but he had to drop out and find a job to support himself and me. He vowed that would never happen to his children. The result is that Joanie and Frank each have a trust of better than one hundred thousand dollars. The interest from these trusts and, in certain instances, even the principal are available to the legal guardian to use in paying for the children's expenses. Suddenly, Adelle was Super-Grandmother, and the next thing I knew, she had petitioned the court to let her have the children.

"I won the first battle. But now..." Anger etched itself into Melinda's features. "I work for a service that supplies temporary secretaries, in order to supplement my earn-ing from my writing so I can raise the children without using their money. I want them to have it for college and to get a start in life. But I know Adelle, and she wants to get her greedy hands on it for herself." Raking a hand through her hair, Melinda shifted her attention to the woods beyond the window. Now came the hard part and she was finding it difficult to proceed. She had been through a lot lately, and having John Medwin laugh her off his property wasn't something she wanted to face.

"This is all very interesting," John said with cool politeness when Melinda's pause lengthened into a silence. "But I don't see how I fit into your domestic situation."

Drawing a terse breath, she met his dark gaze. "It has to do with what happened at the convention. Adelle was having me followed. Apparently she has never given up hope of getting her hands on the money and had decided my behavior at the convention might provide her with some ammunition."

In her mind's eye, Melinda saw the man she had mistaken for a tourist standing in the hall of the hotel toying with his camera when she had come out of Gary's room. "She has pictures of me in my robe and you half-dressed in the doorway of Gary's room. And she has a witness who will swear we spent the night together. She has petitioned the court to reconsider my guardianship and have me declared unfit to raise the children."

"And so you want me to go before the court and swear that nothing happened—that it was all a mistake on the part of an absentminded friend?"

"Not exactly." Suddenly Melinda's nerve broke. This was crazy! "I shouldn't have come here," she blurted out. Pivoting, she headed for the door.

She was on the porch when John's hand closed around her arm, bringing her to an abrupt halt. "Why exactly did you come?"

Again she found herself startled by her awareness of him. The touch of his hand burned through the fabric of her jacket and blouse until her arm felt the contact as if there was no barrier. "Please, let me go." There was an edge of panic in her voice as she tried to pull free.

Ignoring her request, he studied her with purpose. "I want to know what is going on."

"I'm in grave danger of losing my niece and nephew. I refuse to lose my dignity, too," she answered tersely. Jerking free, she continued toward her car.

He caught up with her before she could open the door. Placing a hand on either side of her, he trapped her against the car with his body. "You're not leaving here until I hear the full truth. I realize that's a difficult concept for you, but this time I have to insist."

His closeness was having a distressingly unnerving effect on her already taut nerves. Desperately wanting to get away, Melinda was willing to pay any price. "Judge Craras, he's the judge that has been hearing my case, felt compelled to honor Judy and Kent's wills, but he didn't like the idea of turning their care over to a young, single woman. My lawyer seems to feel the only way to appease him this time would be for you and me to marry. That would give the children a two-parent home, and the pictures taken at the convention could be explained away as a meeting of a secretly engaged couple. Now

I'll be on my way, and you can go inside and have a good laugh about all of this." Her back stiff with pride, she waited for the look of ridicule and for him to free her.

Neither happened. Instead, his expression became shuttered. "How does your boyfriend back home feel about this?"

"There is no boyfriend at home. I was thinking of Frank, my nephew," she answered with defensive honesty.

His jaw twitched as if he had to fight back a smile at her childishness. "And what is there in this marriage for me?"

He was toying with her, making fun of her! "Nothing that would interest you," she snapped. "A wife who isn't your type and who would expect fidelity. And two young children who still have nightmares about being left alone in the world, who have runny noses in the winter, beestings and sunburns in the summer, and still have the chicken pox to look forward to."

"A description like that makes it a hard proposition to turn down," he muttered.

Her hands came up and pushed against him. "You've had your fun. Now let me go!"

Still he didn't free her. "Not yet. It's not every day a man gets such an interesting marriage proposal. I think I should have a chance to consider it."

"I feel foolish enough." Tears of humiliation burned at the back of her eyes but pride held them in check. "You don't have to continue this ridicule to insure that I'll never bother you again. You have my word that when I leave here I'll make every effort to make certain our paths never cross again."

"I'm not ridiculing you," he said gruffly. "I just have a few questions I want answered before I make a decision."

Melinda stared up at him in disbelief. "You're seriously considering my proposal?"

"It's always been a fantasy of mine to rescue a damsel in distress from a fire-breathing dragon." The hint of a smile tilted one corner of his mouth. "Besides, you obviously need someone to look after you. You do seem to be a damsel who gets herself into distressing situations more often than most."

She started to tell him that until he came into her life, she'd been able to handle her problems quite well on her own. But when she looked up into his face, the words died in her throat. His dark eyes were looking into hers with such intense protectiveness that it took her breath away. In the next instant his gaze was once again shuttered. He sees me as an incompetent who needs a keeper, she thought tersely, determined to keep this situation in the proper perspective.

"You mentioned fidelity. Can I assume that you mean this marriage to be real in every sense of the word?" he continued in businesslike tones.

"Judge Craras believes in the sanctity of marriage, and I'm certain Adelle will be keeping an eye on us. Everyone will have to believe that ours is a real and loving marriage and since I don't envision you as a celibate man..." Pausing, she wetted her suddenly dry lips, then finished stiffly, "We would share a bed."

Anger flashed in his eyes. "No sacrifice is too great for your niece and nephew?"

"I didn't mean it that way." Breathing a frustrated sigh, she raked a hand through her hair. "I haven't been thinking too clearly lately. I've been in a panic about losing Joanie and Frank. They're all I have in this world."

Studying the second button of his shirt, she continued shakily, "I convinced myself that proposing an arranged marriage to you was not as ludicrous as it sounded. Considering the divorce rate in this country, I told myself that a marriage based on practical considerations would have as good a chance of surviving as any other. I even had my lawyer prepare a premarital agreement to assure you I wasn't after any of your money." A self-mocking smile played at the corners of her mouth. "I thought I could come up here and present you with this proposal as if it were a business contract. The problem is that in a business contract, both parties are supposed to profit. What I was proposing was a one-sided deal. I would be reaping all the benefits, and marriage, I know, is the last thing you're interested in."

Taking a step back, he stood rigid, his thumbs hooked in the pockets of his jeans. "That's not totally true. I don't have any family, and I've been thinking lately that I would like to have a wife and children. A man needs some roots." He paused for a moment as if making a final decision, then asked, "When do you want this marriage to take place and where would you want to live afterward?"

"I have a home in Wilmington, Delaware. My brother left it to me," she answered. "It's a three-bedroom split-level in the suburbs. It was my parents' home. Judy and Kent lived in it, and after they died I thought the children would adjust better if I continued to raise them there since they'd lived there all their lives. And, of course, there's Harriet. She owns the house next door. She's widowed, and her children are all grown and live out of state. She's like an aunt to the children. She comes over and stays with them whenever I have to be away and baby-sits when I'm doing my part-time secretarial work.''

Stop it! You're rattling on as if you don't have two brain cells to rub together! Melinda reprimanded herself. ''Anyway, I thought we could continue to live there for a little while, at least, until the children have a chance to get accustomed to having you around. I didn't want to force too many changes on them at one time.''

''I suppose Wilmington would be the reasonable choice,'' he conceded. ''The children are, after all, the prime consideration in this marriage.''

There was a hesitation in his manner and Melinda was certain he was searching for a polite but firm way to say he had reconsidered and wasn't interested. Asking him to take on the responsibility of being a father to two small children was a lot. Asking him to give up the beauty and solitude of his wilderness home to live in a split-level in Wilmington, Delaware, was just too much.

Suddenly becoming mobile, he started back toward the house. ''Nevada is the only state I know of where they don't require a waiting period for a marriage license. I'll pack while you book us a flight to Las Vegas," he said over his shoulder.

Melinda felt dizzy. Realizing she had been holding her breath, she gasped for air as she followed. Inside, her legs gave away and she sank into the chair beside the phone table in the hall.

Pausing in front of her, John regarded her grimly. "How much of a surprise am I going to be to your niece and nephew?"

"Before I left, I explained to them that I was going to try to find an uncle for them. I told them I felt it was time for me to marry. They seemed to accept the idea. My brother and sister-in-law were always introducing me to prospective husbands. Probably Joanie and Frank remember their parents trying to marry me off." You're rattling again, she scolded curtly, and swallowed her next sentence.

John nodded to indicate he had heard, then proceeded up the stairs to the loft that served as his bedroom.

Picking up the phone, Melinda punched the buttons for the airport number. Her hands were shaking so badly she got a misdial message and had to punch in the number again. *I can't believe this is happening,* she admitted to herself, close to panic as her call was answered and her vocal cords refused to respond. *This is for Frank and Joanie,* she reminded herself curtly, and found her voice.

Hanging up a few minutes later, she glanced up the stairs toward the loft. *It's never going to work,* her little voice warned.

It has to work, she responded determinedly.

Chapter Four

It was after dark when they arrived in Las Vegas. "I booked a couple of rooms at Caesar's Palace before we left Pennsylvania," John said as they picked up their luggage. "After we check in, I'll buy you dinner and then we can get a good night's rest."

A while later, sitting across the table from him, Melinda could not relax. She sipped a glass of wine hoping it would ease her tension, but she might as well have been drinking water. She tried concentrating on the variety of people seated around them, but the couple that held her attention were an elderly man, obviously wealthy, and a young, very attractive woman. Probably one of the showgirls, she decided. The kind of woman John would normally be with, her little voice added, setting her nerves on edge.

"I read one of your books." John broke the uncomfortably long silence that had fallen between them. "It was interesting. I wasn't certain who the murderer was until the last chapter."

"I read one of yours," she admitted, her muscles tensing even more as she recalled some of the descriptive passages dealing with the tall, leggy females Nicolus Blade always bedded.

"And what did you think?" he questioned coolly when the pause following this admission lengthened into a silence.

"I was intimidated," she answered, frowning down at the plate of food she had been playing with rather than eating. "Your women are all so gorgeous. Like those two women who hung all over you at the convention." The last words brought a heated flush to her face. She had not meant to mention Lanie and her blond friend or the female characters in his books. But they had been on her mind all day, and the combination of fatigue and wine had loosened her tongue.

"The women I write about are meant to satisfy the most common fantasies men have about what is physically beautiful. It sells books. My personal tastes are more varied." With a slightly self-conscious smile, he added, "Lanie and Sandie are professional models hired by my agent. He thought they would enhance my image."

Startled by this revelation, Melinda glanced toward her dinner companion. "They certainly seemed to be enjoying your company," she said with a strong edge of disbelief, recalling the hostile look the blonde had shot at her on the veranda.

"Women do occasionally find my company interesting," he replied dryly.

Behind his closed expression she sensed anger and doubt. She knew he, too, must be reconsidering his decision to marry her. The thought of losing her niece and nephew terrified her, but at the same time she was finding it harder and harder to convince herself this marriage could work. Her stomach knotted and nerves sent a wave of nausea surging through her. "I'm really not hungry," she said. "I think I'll go to my room and get some rest."

Impatience shadowed his features. Lifting his hand, he started to signal for the waiter.

"Please." She caught his arm. "Stay and finish your meal."

Lowering his hand, he said simply, "I'll pick you up at eight for breakfast."

She could feel his eyes on her as she wound her way through the tables and out of the restaurant. She knew he was angry and he had every right to be. She had been the one who had come to him with this marriage proposal, and now she was acting as if she were going to a funeral.

All the way back to her room, she half expected him to catch up with her and call the whole thing off. She was trapped into this for the sake of her niece and nephew. He wasn't. But he didn't catch up with her and he didn't come knocking on her door.

Lying in bed tossing and turning, fighting for sleep to come, she wondered if he would actually be at her door at eight the next morning. "I'd better not count on it," she told herself, and there was almost a sense of relief in those words. But the relief was quickly replaced by panic when she thought of Joanie and Frank. When sleep finally came the hour was well past midnight.

Melinda awoke at seven feeling as exhausted as before she'd finally fallen asleep. After showering, she dressed carefully in a lightweight cotton dress and added extra makeup in an attempt to hide the dark circles under her eyes. Then, unable to sit, she paced the floor of her room, glancing at her watch continually. One minute to eight. She had almost convinced herself it would be for the best if he didn't show up, when a knock sounded on her door. Opening it, she found John dressed in a pair of slacks and a short-sleeved shirt. His face showed no emotion.

"A bride should have flowers," he said matter-of-factly, handing her a florist's box. Inside was a bouquet of white roses.

"Thank you," she managed, wondering what was going through his mind but unable to bring herself to ask. He had to be having doubts.

On the way to the chapel, they stopped at a jeweler's and purchased a matching pair of gold bands. She insisted on paying for his. "For luck," she explained.

He gave her a we're-going-to-need-it look and her doubts grew stronger.

At the door of the chapel, her conscience would allow her to go no farther. "Are you certain you want to go through with this?" she asked, giving him a final chance to back out. "I really will understand if you've changed your mind."

"Oh, I'm certain I want to marry you," he answered firmly. "The question is, are you still certain you want to marry me?"

The word *no* formed on the tip of her tongue, but it was a surprisingly firm "Yes" that came out.

Nodding, he started to open the door of the chapel, but she caught his arm. "I have one other question," she heard herself saying hesitantly.

Releasing the handle of the door, he studied her face for a moment. "What is it?"

Don't push your luck, her inner voice warned, but she paid it no heed. The question had been nagging her and had to be asked. "Why are you marrying me?" John raised a bemused eyebrow as if to say he'd already answered that question. "I mean the real reason—not that stuff about fighting dragons and wanting a wife and kids. I don't believe in self-sacrificing chivalry. It only exists in Arthurian legends."

"Melinda, what a very cynical view of the world," he admonished.

Ignoring the interruption, she continued stiffly. "And if you wanted to marry, you could have your choice of women."

His expression became grim. "I know what it's like for a child to be raised in an environment where he or she isn't really wanted. Gary expended quite a bit of energy telling me what a wonderful mother and homemaker you are, how you have devoted yourself to your niece and nephew. And you've proven to me that you care more for them than for yourself." A bitter smile tilted one corner of his mouth. "Children need that kind of love. I don't want to see your niece and nephew taken away from you."

For a moment, Melinda glimpsed the lonely, angry little boy who had been abandoned at the doors of an orphanage. Reaching up, she touched his face with a gentle caress. "Gary told me you had a difficult childhood."

"Gary overdramatizes," he growled, stepping back from her touch. "Your pity isn't necessary."

Dropping her hand to her side, she watched his face close up again. "Will you accept my gratitude?" she asked, wondering if he ever let anyone inside the barrier he kept around his inner self.

"We'll both benefit," he replied in businesslike tones. "You have agreed to have my children." Before she could respond, he opened the door and stepped aside to allow her to enter ahead of him.

For half a second she hesitated, then she stepped over the threshold.

A cold shiver of doubt shook Melinda as the minister pronounced them man and wife, then John's lips met hers for the traditional kiss. It was only a light brush, but it sent her blood surging.

"I've made reservations for us to fly back to Pennsylvania," he informed her as they walked out of the chapel and into the Las Vegas heat. "I need to pack more than this." His gaze swung to the small leather satchel he had brought with him, then back to Melinda. "And I thought it might be a good idea if we spent a couple of days together, just the two of us, to get to know each other."

"When I called last night, Harriet told me everything was going well and she wouldn't expect me home for a few days," Melinda replied, her heart beating rapidly, half with fear and half with anticipation.

Relief registered on John's face. "Good. I can use a couple of days to get used to the idea of being married before having to assume the role of uncle and parent."

The sun was setting over the tops of the mountains when, several hours later, John lifted her into his arms and carried her over the threshold of his house. During the flight they had talked very little. John had slept most of the way. Melinda had tried to sleep but had finally given up the futile effort. Too keyed up to even work on the plotting of her latest book, she had been reduced to skimming every magazine on the plane. She was sorely tempted to borrow the child's comic books from the seat across the aisle by the time the pilot had finally announced they would be landing soon. Then there had been the drive from the airport to the house. She recited every story of the least interest she'd read on the plane to John. She knew she was babbling but she was too tense to be silent. Now they were at his home, and the rock in the pit of her stomach finally brought silence to her lips as he set her down gently in the entrance hall.

As he stared down at her, his expression shifted to an impatient frown. "For goodness' sake, I'm not going to rape you."

"I appreciate that," she muttered. Then with a self-mocking smile, she said apologetically, "I'm just a little tense."

The scowl on his face darkened further. "You're making me feel like the big, bad wolf stalking Little Red Riding Hood."

"I don't mean to. I'm sure a warm shower will relax me," she assured him.

But the shower didn't help. Seeing herself in the bathroom mirror only increased her fears of inadequacy. She lacked a good four inches of measuring up to *his* storybook fantasies, and certainly no one would ever describe her as having a cool, sophisticated aura. She was more the plain old girl-next-door type. Wrapping her old terry-cloth robe around her, she left the sanctity of the bathroom and climbed the stairs to the loft.

John was there and—to her relief—still dressed. On a small round table set along the railing that kept the occupants of the loft from falling into the living room was a plate of cheese and crackers. "I thought something to eat might soothe your nerves," he said.

She forced a smile. "Thank you." Attempting to appear nonchalant, she popped a bite of cheese into her mouth as she crossed to her suitcase and took out her hair dryer.

"You can plug it in here." He nodded toward an outlet near the bed.

"Thanks," she managed as she swallowed the cheese and felt it hit her stomach like a small stone. Her hand was shaking as she plugged in the hair dryer. She had never been this undressed in front of a man before.

He's your husband, she chided herself.

He's a stranger, her little voice countered in her defense. Trying not to think, she seated herself on the edge of the bed and loosened the towel from around her hair.

"Let me do that." Taking the dryer from her, John began to comb through her hair with his free hand, separating the wet strands so the dryer could work more effectively. A warm tingling spread through her as his fingers worked from her forehead over her scalp. On the next sweep, he started at her neck. Warm currents like tiny sparks of electricity raced through her. His legs brushed against hers and her awareness of him grew so intense she trembled.

Abruptly he snapped the hair dryer off. "You didn't have to be afraid of me," he said curtly. Dropping the hair dryer on the bed, he added, "I'm going to take a cold shower."

She told herself she should stop him and tell him he had misinterpreted her tremble. But before she could convince herself to say something, he was gone.

"Coward!" she muttered angrily, picking up the hair dryer and switching it back on. "Your pride's going to ruin this marriage before it has a chance to start!" But she didn't want to make a fool of herself; she knew she was nothing like his fantasies. Her jaw hardened. She needed to develop a positive attitude. "Think tall and sophisticated!" she ordered herself.

Putting the hair dryer aside, she stood and studied herself critically in the mirror. "Thinking tall and sophisticated isn't going to change my image. However..."

Determination glittering in her eyes, she brushed her hair and applied a light layer of makeup. Now, what to wear. Neither of the two nightgowns she had thrown into her suitcase could, by any stretch of the imagination, be considered sexy. She'd come here in a sudden surge of panic at the idea of losing the children, and she hadn't thought past the proposal. As her mind traveled through his books, a light suddenly flashed; his women were always putting on their boyfriends' shirts!

Going to his closet, Melinda found a white cotton shirt with long sleeves and a button-down collar. Shedding her robe, she slipped it on. The effect on her senses was startling. She had worn a man's shirt before; she used to wear her brother's old discarded ones when she was gardening or cleaning. But they had never made her feel like this. As the fabric of John's shirt brushed against her skin, it awakened a sensuous femininity within her.

Rolling up the sleeves until her hands and lower arms were visible, she began to button it, leaving the top four open. Her breasts were full and the visible cleavage was nothing to be ashamed about. Unfolding the collar, she refolded it so the back remained up. As it brushed against the back of her neck, a strong sense of John's presence filled her.

A heated flush warmed her body and a wanting began to grow inside her.

"Now for a little height," she said aloud, forcing her mind back to her original objective. From her suitcase, she pulled out the pair of gray four-inch heels. Slipping them on, she again surveyed herself in the mirror. "Just keep thinking tall and sophisticated," she reminded herself tersely, and with one final stroke of the brush through her hair, she went down to the living room.

The fireplace was set, ready to be lit to take the chill off the cool mountain night. Striking one of the long matches, she set the kindling ablaze. Next she switched off all the lights so that only the glow from the fire illuminated the interior of the room.

Now where should she be when he first saw her? Looking around, fighting down a sudden wave of panic, she considered lying on the rug in front of the fire with her head propped up on one hand and a why-don't-you-join-me? look on her face. But that would destroy the tall effect she was hoping to create with the heels.

Pacing across the room, she came to a halt in front of the fire. As she stared into the flames, her insecurities again assailed her. He was probably going to laugh at her attempt to appear sexy.

"Do you mind telling me why you're wearing one of my shirts and a pair of very uncomfortable-looking shoes? I could have sworn you were the type of woman who wouldn't go anywhere without a sensible nightgown and slippers."

She swung around at the sound of his voice. John stood halfway across the room. His hair, still damp from his shower, looked almost blue-black as it glistened in the firelight. His only covering was a towel draped around his hips.

He was laughing at her. "Nicolus Blade would never ask a woman a question like that!" she retorted, her back straightening with pride.

"Nicolus Blade hardly ever notices what his women are wearing," he countered.

Defiantly, she met the brown of his eyes. But the amusement she had expected to find wasn't there. Instead, he was watching her in a way that heated the warm sensuous glow wearing his shirt had produced to a slow simmer. "I was trying to think tall and sophisticated," she confessed huskily.

"I prefer my women barefoot," he said, remaining at a distance.

Catching her bottom lip between her teeth, she kicked the heels off toward a darkened corner of the room.

John moved closer. "I hope you realize that you're starting something a cold shower isn't going to stop," he warned.

Reaching out, she let her hands rest on his shoulders. Hot currents ran through her, and the simmer became a boil. "Stopping is the last thing I have on my mind," she promised.

"I'm glad to hear that." His hands found her waist, then moved upward to cup her breasts.

Gasping as her nipples hardened and her blood seemed to turn to molten lava, she moved her own hands up over his shoulders and to his neck.

His mouth found hers and the wanting grew inside of her until she felt the need to be possessed by him with an intensity that shocked her. It was like a hunger that threatened to kill her if it wasn't satisfied. A little frightened by the strength of her awakened desire, she stiffened.

As if their senses were intertwined, she felt his anger surge at this sign of withdrawal. Instinctively she raised up on tiptoe to add her own strength to the kiss. At the same time, she swayed against him, apologizing with her body, letting him know she didn't want him to stop.

Deserting her mouth, he trailed kisses along her neck to the valley between her breasts as he unfastened the buttons of the shirt. When the last button came free, he straightened a little away from her. Then slowly, as if he wanted to savor the moment, he slipped the garment from her shoulders while his eyes traveled with masculine inspection along the lines of her body.

Fear that he would be disappointed again assailed her. Shakily, she forced herself to look into his face. The wanting she saw there vanquished her fear in its flames.

As if some primitive instinct controlled them, her hands moved along the length of his body, over his hips and down the strong columns of his legs as she lowered herself to the floor. Her forwardness amazed her, but it felt right to touch him, and telling herself that he was her husband, she did not fight the seductive instincts that guided her touch.

Lowering himself beside her, John discarded the towel. For a moment panic again swept over her. She had always heard there was pain the first time. Then he touched her and her need was too strong for any fear to stop her.

She gasped at the newness of possession. The pain was there, but it passed as he caressed and kissed her until all else vanished from her senses except for the intensity of their mutual desire.

Afterward, lying snuggled beside him, she opened her eyes to find him watching her guardedly.

"I didn't hurt you, did I?" he asked gruffly.

Levering herself on an arm so she could place a light kiss on his mouth, she said quietly, "No, you didn't hurt me."

He continued to regard her, but his eyes were unreadable. "You should have warned me. I never expected you to be a virgin."

Defiance flashed through her and her body stiffened. "I didn't think that was something a woman was supposed to apologize for."

She started to move away from him, but his hold on her tightened. "I didn't mean it as an accusation," he said softly. "It was more of a wonderment. If I believe all the statistics I read in magazines, twenty-seven-year-old virgins are almost nonexistent."

He was making fun of her. "Maybe you shouldn't believe all you read," she suggested dryly, again trying to pull free.

Shifting his body, he pinned her beneath him. "If I tell you that I found making love to you one of the most exciting experiences of my life, will you forgive my musings about virginity and stop trying to get away?"

His body on top of hers was reawakening her desire. "I was beginning to believe I was frigid," she confessed. "I never thought I would ever really want a man." The slow burning was now becoming a renewed flame. "I never knew it could feel like such an essential need." Her tongue came out to moisten her lips as her hands moved caressingly over his chest.

"I'm a little surprised myself," he admitted, kissing her shoulder lightly.

Instinctively, her body arched toward his. "It also seems to be instantly habit-forming," she murmured, nuzzling the hollow of his neck.

John laughed softly. "Nicolus Blade never had it this good," he assured her as his mouth met hers with a renewed demand for possession.

Chapter Five

Early-morning sunlight was streaming in the windows when Melinda slowly opened her eyes the next morning. When the fire in the fireplace downstairs had died, she and John had come up to the loft to crawl under the heavy down comforter on his bed for warmth. A gentle smile curled her lips as she saw his dark-haired head on the pillow next to hers.

A feeling of fulfillment washed over her. She reached out to touch the rich, thick locks of hair, but just as the contact was about to be made, she drew back her hand. Memories of the first morning she'd woken in the same room with him came rushing back, followed by a sharp reminder of why she was in his bed now. Theirs was a marriage of convenience! Still, she could not deny the strong currents of emotion running through her at this moment. You're in lust, not love, she told herself firmly, and if you don't want to get hurt, you'll keep that in mind.

Her jaw set with firm resolve, she climbed quietly out of bed. Her first instinct was to reach for the discarded shirt. But as her hands brushed against the fabric and sensuous stirrings ignited within her, she forced herself to choose her old terry-cloth bathrobe instead. She couldn't think totally rationally with John's shirt on, and she needed a clear head to get her emotions back into the proper perspective.

Down in the kitchen, she found the coffee and coffeepot and started it perking. A porch with a protective roof and a waist-high railing spanned the length of the back of the house. Munching on a piece of cheese, she stepped out onto the porch. A fresh, wood-scented breeze greeted her. Perching on the railing near one of the posts supporting the roof, she leaned against the sturdy, square column and stared out at the tranquil wooded scene that seemed to stretch forever around her.

"Good morning." John's voice interrupted the early-morning silence.

Turning toward the door, she saw him coming out carrying two mugs of coffee. He was shirtless and barefoot, wearing only an old pair of faded jeans, and the immediacy of her body's reaction startled her. "Morning," she returned levelly, swinging her gaze back to the woods. She was unwilling to take a chance he might read the extent of her weakness toward him in her eyes.

"Cream, no sugar," he said, extending one of the mugs toward her.

Surprise that he'd remembered registered on her face as she glanced back toward him. "That's right."

Amusement at her surprise brought a playful smile to his face that started her heart pounding erratically. Accepting the mug, she again shifted her attention toward the woods. A prickling on her neck told her he was watching her and she felt a sudden desperate need to make small talk—to cover the emotions he was stirring. "It's very peaceful here," she said with forced casualness.

Seating himself in one of the porch chairs, he rested his feet on the rail. "I found this land when I was working as a lumberjack. I bought it and promised myself that one day I would come back here and live. About five years later, my writing began to pay off and I couldn't think of a better place to work."

"I'm afraid that, compared to this, you're going to feel as if you're living in the middle of total chaos when you come home with me," Melinda said, a note of anxiety mingling with the apology in her voice.

"I wrote my first book while working as a deckhand on a rusty freighter and my second while I was a member of a round-the-clock, oil-drilling crew. I'm used to working in the midst of noise and confusion," he assured her. Taking a drink of his coffee, he shifted his gaze to the trees lining the clearing. "Tell me about Joanie and Frank."

A softness came into Melinda's eyes. "They're good children. Not perfect," she amended quickly, "but basically warm and loving and well behaved. Joanie is six—petite, very pretty—a blonde like her mother, with blue eyes. She looks like a fragile china doll, and ever since her parents' deaths she sometimes gets a frightened look in her eyes that makes her seem even more vulnerable. But she doesn't get it as often now as she used to.

"Then there's Frank." A loving smile curled the corners of Melinda's mouth. "He's only seven but he's appointed himself the man of the house. Ever since he was a baby, he's behaved like an adult. He walks and talks like his father, and with his brown hair and eyes, he looks like Kent, too. He even has Kent's protective attitude toward us females of the family. That doesn't mean that he and Joanie don't quarrel—they have royal battles. But if an outsider picks a fight with his sister, he's there to defend her to the death." A mildly anxious look entered Melinda's eyes. "He's also a bit protective of me, but I don't think he'll give you any trouble.

"I lived with my brother and his wife until I finished secretarial school, then I moved out. Frank had been born and Joanie was on the way. I felt Kent and Judy needed the house for their own family, and I wanted to be on my own. But they worried about me, and as I mentioned before, their solution was to find me a suitable husband—which they attempted to do with gusto. I was lucky my brother and sister-in-law had high standards. As it was, I think I must have been introduced to at least a third of all the eligible men in Wilmington." Suddenly embarrassed that she'd mentioned these futile attempts to see her wed, she finished stiffly, "Anyway, I think it's ingrained in the children's brains that I should be married."

"I have to admit I'm surprised you hadn't found Mr. Right," John said as his gaze traveled over her. "You strike me as the basic domestic type—and you're pretty enough to have your pick."

"I suppose I was looking for that special spark," she replied, then wished she had kept her mouth shut as a cynical smile played across his face.

"The forever-after kind of love, as found in all the fairy tales your mother read to you," he said.

"Something like that," she admitted tightly. Tired of being the brunt of his sarcastic amusement, she decided it was time to turn the tables. "You know all about me. All I know about you is rumors."

His expression again becoming unreadable, he turned his attention to a rabbit feeding along the perimeter of the lawn. "There isn't much to tell. I was raised in an orphanage. It wasn't a bad place. It was run by some nuns. They didn't have much money so I left when I was sixteen. I lied about my age and found a job working for a lumber company. I cut trees from Maine to Pennsylvania, then decided I wanted to see the big city and migrated to New York. From there I moved from one job to another. I read a lot—then discovered I had a knack for writing."

Melinda studied his taut profile. There was an air of loneliness about him that pulled at her heart. "Have you ever tried to find..." she began, only to have the question die in her throat when his gaze swung toward her and she saw the bitterness in his eyes.

"Have I tried to find my mother?" He spoke the words as if they tasted of poison.

The intensity of his anger frightened her. Still, she had brought the subject up. She could not let it rest without trying to ease the pain he was so determined not to admit. "It's obvious your abandonment still bothers you," she said in a reasoning voice. "But your mother probably felt she had no choice. Maybe if you found her—"

"I found her," he interrupted caustically. "A few years ago, after my books began to sell well and I had some time and cash, I started looking. Actually, it wasn't too difficult. I started with one of the older nuns who had been at the orphanage when I was brought in. Normally she wouldn't have told me anything, but she'd always liked me, and through the years I had sent what money I could to help them out. So she talked to me. She didn't know a great deal. My mother

had used a false name when she had signed
me in. But the sister did know my mother
had been part of a commune a few miles
away. The commune wasn't there anymore
but the man who still lived on the land had
been a member. He knew my mother's
maiden name and that she had relatives in
Cleveland, Ohio.''

Cynicism replaced the bitterness in his
voice. ''I hired a detective to do the searching after that. It took him a couple of
months, but he finally came up with a name
and address. I decided to call before I went
to the house. My darling mother nearly
panicked. She begged me not to come to her
home and said she would meet with me the
next day. She came, driving a Mercedes and
wearing enough diamonds to choke a horse.
She admitted to being my mother, then went
on to explain that my father had also been a
member of the commune. They were both
very young when they joined, she was sixteen and he was barely seventeen. Both had
run away from home. Fatherhood was the
last thing my father wanted. He left the
commune before I was born.'' Pausing, John

ran a hand through his hair in an agitated manner.

"My mother stuck it out for another three years, then realized it wasn't the life for her. She preferred the luxury of her middle-class home. However, I presented a problem. She didn't want to go back with an illegitimate child. She wanted to resume her life where she'd left off, which would have been impossible with me to care for. So she turned me over to the nuns. She told me she was glad life had turned out well for me—then she begged me not to reveal her secret. She said it would ruin her life if her husband and her two legitimate children found out about me. She explained that I would be an embarrassment to all of them, not to mention her parents and other family members." He shrugged as if shaking off memories that were better forgotten.

Slipping off the railing, Melinda walked around behind his chair and wrapped her arms around his shoulders in a mothering gesture. "I'm sorry," she said, fighting to keep her voice level. "It's her loss."

Unwrapping her arms, he rose and faced her with the shuttered look she was beginning to know so well. "In many ways I'm grateful for my upbringing. It has taught me to count only on myself." The warning not to try to get too close to him was clear.

And if you're smart you'll heed that warning, her little voice advised.

Moving toward the house, he said coolly, "I have some business calls to make and packing to do." Pausing with his hand on the doorknob, he turned back. "You're the only person I've told the truth to. I don't want the story to go any further. The rumors suit me just fine."

"Yes, of course. I won't repeat it," she assured him.

With a nod that he accepted her word, he continued into the house.

For a long moment, Melinda stood staring at the chair he had so recently occupied. He was determined to remain an island unto himself. Her jaw tightened as she admitted to herself that she'd hoped their relationship might deepen through the years. Now she had no hope for that.

He's helping me keep Joanie and Frank, she reminded herself. In return I'll provide him with heirs. It's a reasonable arrangement and built on more practical grounds than most marriages. If she didn't expect more than what was promised, she wouldn't get hurt. "I won't," she said, as if saying the words aloud would give them more credibility. And with the promise firmly in mind, she went inside to dress and offer her assistance with his packing.

He was on the phone when she passed through the hall. "I'm going to have to cancel out on our week up here," he was saying apologetically. "But I'll leave a key in the usual place, and you can come up and enjoy the peace and quiet on your own if you want."

Melinda's stomach twisted. You knew he had women friends, she told herself curtly, and you can't have believed that he would spend all of his time alone up here. Angry that the call had affected her so strongly, she hurried up the stairs to the loft to find her clothes. But as she took a quick shower before dressing, his promise to "leave a key in the usual place" continued to nag at her.

Returning to the loft, she found him sorting through his drawers and closets, tossing the clothes he wanted to pack onto the bed.

"Can I help?" she offered, fighting to hide the hostile edge that threatened to creep into her voice.

Pausing, he glanced toward her. Then, with a nod of his head, he indicated the empty luggage lined up and waiting. "The clothes go in the two large suitcases and the suit bag. I'll pack my files in the medium-size one."

An anger she didn't want to feel urged her to stuff the clothes into the bags haphazardly. But ordering herself to behave responsibly, she folded them carefully and packed them neatly.

He was downstairs sorting through his files when she finished. Snapping the suitcase shut, she momentarily debated her next move. The anger she was trying to suppress refused to go away. Her eyes fell on the bed, and she had a sudden mental image of Sandie lying there. The models might have been hired for the convention, but she knew either of them gladly would have accepted an invitation to come here. You're acting like a jealous woman, her inner voice chided.

Picking up the large suitcase, she carried it downstairs and set it next to the door with a loud thud.

"I'll carry those down," John called out from his study.

"I really don't mind," she tossed back.

Practically bolting upstairs, she was picking up the suit bag when John's hand closed over hers. Releasing the bag, she turned to face him. "I really don't need any help," she assured him. "I'm used to lifting and carrying."

Ignoring her assurance, he studied her grimly. "I think we'd better discuss your anger before you strain a muscle or start breaking things. Are you upset because I was honest with you? Were you expecting more from this marriage than what we agreed?"

She shrugged her shoulders with schooled indifference. "Don't be ridiculous. I'm not angry with you."

"You're not a good liar." The scowl on his face deepened. "I know a woman's controlled anger when I see it. So come clean, Melinda. What female sensitivity have I injured?"

His cynical, patronizing indulgence only added fire to her growing anger. "You have not injured any of my *female sensitivities,*" she responded icily. "I am only concerned about losing my niece and nephew. I didn't mean to eavesdrop, but I heard you on the phone telling your friend she could use this place at her convenience...that the key would be in the usual place. If anyone finds out about other women having free access to your home, they're likely to use the information to discredit our marriage."

He regarded her musingly. "The conversation you overheard was between me and my agent, who happens to be a man."

I warned you not to overreact, her little voice scolded, as an embarrassed flush built from her neck upward. Wanting only to escape, she reached for a suitcase. "Now that that's settled, we'd better get back to the packing," she said stiffly.

Catching her hand before it reached the luggage, he carried it to his shoulder. "Your eyes glisten with the most fascinating fire when you're angry," he said, kissing the tip of her nose. Capturing her other hand, he placed it on his other shoulder. "I can finish packing in five minutes." Leaning forward, he kissed the sensitive cord of her neck. "And since we only have this one day of privacy, let's not waste it."

Melinda wanted to resist. She wanted to show some coolness. She wanted to prove to him and to herself that she had some immunity to him. But as his lips found hers, her arms wound around his neck and her body melted against his. I'm just responding to a basic human need; I've waited too long and now I'm catching up on lost time, she assured herself as he began to unbutton her blouse. Her whole body trembled with an intensity of wanting that his touch so easily aroused.

Her hands were reaching for the snap on his jeans when the ringing of the phone interrupted. She felt his hesitation and with her fingers lying inactive on the snap, she looked up into his face.

"Maybe it will stop," he said gruffly. But it didn't. "It's probably one of the business calls I made earlier being returned," he explained apologetically as he released her. Placing a light kiss on her lips, he ordered, "Don't forget where we were. I'll be right back," and with a disgruntled groan, he went downstairs to answer it.

"It's for you," he called up the loft a moment later.

The caller had to be Harriet. The number was unlisted. Melinda had had to call Gary to get it, and she had given it only to Harriet. Besides, only Harriet knew she was here. Frantic that something had happened to one of the children, she dashed down the stairs and breathed an urgent "Hello" into the phone.

"I called to warn you," Harriet's unhappy voice came over the line. "Adelle came by to visit the children today, and Joanie let it slip that you'd gone and gotten married to Mr. Medwin. Adelle was furious. She started ranting and raving about how she was going to get a court order and have the children taken out of this house immediately. She said that her grandchildren were not going to be raised by a man who wrote lurid books."

"Thanks," Melinda said with a tired sigh. It had been silly to hope this marriage would stop Adelle. She took a few minutes to talk to the children, then hung up.

"Bad news?" John asked. He had remained beside her, watching her face while she talked.

"Adelle found out about the marriage, but it hasn't stopped her." Sinking onto the chair beside the phone, she placed a call to her lawyer.

"Medwin's books are not considered lurid or pornographic by the general public. In fact, I happen to know that Judge Craras reads them all the time," Philip assured her. "If there was any way Adelle could have used them to get the children, I would never have suggested a marriage."

Thanking him, she hung up.

"What did he say?" John questioned.

"He says that your Nicolus Blade books, while they may not earn you a Pulitzer prize, aren't considered lurid or pornographic and will not cause the court to rule against your becoming a father to Joanie and Frank," she answered, trying to force a lightness into her voice.

Folding his arms in front of him, he leaned against the wall and studied her with concern. "You don't look totally convinced."

Drawing a deep breath, she met his steady gaze. "I just don't trust Adelle. I'm never certain what she'll try next."

"Would you feel better if we returned to Wilmington today?"

"Yes," she admitted.

His manner became businesslike. "Then we will. After all, you keeping your niece and nephew is the main reason for this marriage." Glancing at his watch, he added, "We should be able to have the car packed before noon. There's a little cafe down the road a few miles. We'll stop there for lunch. It's going to be a long drive and I need my nourishment." Before Melinda could respond, he'd returned to his study and she heard him tossing files into the suitcase.

In spite of her strong need to be with Joanie and Frank, Melinda felt a deep regret that she and John wouldn't have this one day of privacy. Then, chiding herself for caring so much about having time alone with him, she went upstairs and repacked her suitcase.

Chapter Six

Stopping only for short breaks and dinner, they arrived in Wilmington a little after ten. Harriet was asleep in front of the television. Switching off the set, Melinda woke her gently.

"I told the children they could meet their new uncle in the morning," Harriet explained through a wide yawn as she sleepily inspected John. "But I decided I would wait up so I could go home. Your guest room is nice. But I prefer my own bed. Besides, I thought you should have a strictly family breakfast tomorrow." For the first time, she tore her gaze away from John and glanced toward Melinda. "Even as a child you always had a sense of purpose. When you said you were going to do something you usually managed to accomplish it. But I must say, even I'm surprised at your success this time. If I thought I could go off looking for a husband and come back with something like him—" Harriet smiled toward John "—I'd be packed and gone by dawn."

"I really appreciate you looking after the children," Melinda said, finally able to get a word in.

"I'm just sorry Adelle butted in and sent you scurrying home." Harriet shook her head in self-reproach. "I should never have let her inside this house, but you know how pushy she can be. And, of course, she came with a toy for each of the children. She reminds me of the wicked witch with her poisoned apples in Snow White. I wish—"

Melinda was in no mood to discuss Adelle. "It's really late," she interrupted.

"You're right." Harriet nodded and began stuffing her knitting into its bag. "I'm sure you two are tired and I know I am. So I'll just toddle home."

"I'll see you to your door." John spoke for the first time as he followed Harriet out into the hall.

"There's really no need." The older woman flushed with pleasure at this polite gesture.

"I insist." Reaching around her, he opened the door and waited for her to exit ahead of him.

Sending Melinda an I'm-really-impressed smile, Harriet waved good-night and stepped outside.

Going upstairs, Melinda peeked in on the children. She wanted to give them each a big hug, but she knew it would wake them, and she needed some rest before she faced introducing them to their new uncle.

Coming out into the hall from Joanie's room, she found John waiting with his luggage.

"This is our room," she said, opening the door of the master bedroom and stepping aside to allow him to enter with the suitcases.

"Is Adelle really as formidable as Harriet paints her?" he questioned, setting the bags down.

"I'm sure you'll have the opportunity to find out for yourself fairly soon," Melinda answered tiredly.

"That sounds almost like a warning."

"You did say you'd always wanted to confront a fire-breathing dragon," she reminded him. Then, stifling a yawn, she said, "Could we not discuss Adelle anymore tonight? I'm exhausted, and I don't want her to be the last thing on my mind when I drift off to sleep."

Tilting her chin upward, John placed a light kiss on her lips. "I have no intention of allowing Adelle to be the last thing on your mind when you drift off to sleep."

Melinda awoke the next morning to the sound of whispering young voices. Opening one eye, she found Joanie and Frank watching her. Smiling, she opened both eyes and spread her arms. "How about a welcome-home hug?" she said as they both ran into her embrace.

"Is that him?" Joanie questioned in a loud whisper, her eyes traveling past Melinda to John's bulk on the other side of the bed.

"Yes, that's your uncle John," Melinda confirmed in a returning whisper.

"Frank walked around and looked at him," Joanie confided, her expression becoming anxious. "He said he looks sort of like a bear... a grizzly bear. You know, the kind that eat people."

"Well, he does," Frank said, defending his description as Melinda glanced toward him with a reproving frown.

Turning her attention back toward Joanie, Melinda smiled reassuringly. "He's very gentle. You have nothing to worry about." A hand moved playfully along the back of her leg, letting her know that John was awake and listening. Fighting down a giggle, she kicked at him gently to warn him to stop.

Rewarding her with a little pat on her seat, he raised himself up on one elbow and looked over her to the children.

Joanie took a step back, but Frank remained firmly rooted.

Focusing his attention on his new niece, John smiled and winked. Joanie continued to regard him dubiously and kept her distance.

"That usually works with women," he mused playfully as he winked again. "My ego is taking a real beating this morning."

Still Joanie kept her distance.

"Harriet says we should be glad to have you in the family and we should treat you nicely," Frank said, breaking his silence. He didn't look or sound as if he was fully convinced Harriet was right. But with his back stiff with courage, he took a step forward and extended his hand toward John.

Reaching over Melinda, John accepted the handshake, his large hand completely engulfing the smaller one.

As Frank's hand was released, he took a step back. A smile of triumph, as if he'd faced the beast and survived to tell about it, spread over his face. Then, catching his sister's hand, he pulled her toward the door. "We'll go down and watch television until it's time for breakfast," he told Melinda with an air of authority. Pushing Joanie out of the room ahead of him, he closed the door behind them.

John frowned with concern at the closed door. "I seem to have made a rather frightening first impression."

"You have a tendency to do that," Melinda replied, again recalling her first encounter with him. "But they'll get used to you. You just have to give them time." Tossing off the covers, she headed for the bathroom. "And I have to give them breakfast."

She was frying the bacon when Frank came into the kitchen. "Our new uncle needs some paper towels," he said in his I'm-here-on-an-important-mission voice.

"What does he need them for?" she asked. "Did someone spill something?" It was a conditioned question. The children were always trying to clean up messes on their own and making bigger messes she eventually had to clean.

"I don't know what he wants them for." Frank lowered his voice to a conspiratorial whisper. "Joanie dared me to go in and look at him again. I was real quiet. He had his jeans on and was making the bed. Then he looked up and saw me and asked me if I would get him some towels."

Keeping an eye on the bacon, Melinda tore off the towels.

"He also wants a pair of scissors. Can I get the ones you use for sewing?" Frank asked, accepting the handful of towels. "I gave him my school scissors but he said they weren't sturdy enough."

"Yes, go ahead." Watching Frank practically fly out of the room, Melinda wondered what John was up to. Her curiosity urged her to go see, but the bacon would burn if she left it, and this was the first meal she'd ever cooked for John. She did want it to be eatable.

On his way back upstairs, Frank must have made a detour down to the playroom to give Joanie the details of his latest adventure. Turning the bacon, Melinda heard two pairs of feet scurrying up the stairs. I'm afraid John didn't realize what he was getting into when he agreed to this marriage, she thought frantically. But she had warned him.

Fifteen minutes later, she put the cooked bacon in the oven and went in search of the children. She knew they hadn't come back downstairs. Upstairs, she glanced into their rooms to find them vacant. Coming to the master bedroom, she looked inside to find Joanie standing behind Frank, who was standing in the doorway of the bathroom.

Joanie glanced toward her as she entered. "Uncle John is cutting off his beard and mustache," she said, her voice holding an edge of awe.

"He's what?" Coming to a halt behind the children, Melinda saw John. He had trimmed his beard and mustache down to stubble. "You didn't have to do that," she said tightly.

"It's too hot for a beard and mustache in town in the summer," he replied, setting aside the scissors and picking up the hair-filled paper towels from the sink. Dumping them into the trash basket, he spread out another layer of towels on top of the sink and, after wetting his face, smeared shaving cream over the heavy stubble that remained. Melinda watched with as much fascination as the children as he shaved off the remaining hair, wiping the razor on the paper towels so as not to clog the sink.

Finally rinsing and drying his face, he turned to face them. "Well?"

Frank was the first to respond. "I liked you better with the beard," he stated firmly. Then, grabbing his sister's hand, he said, "Come on, it's time for *Tom and Jerry*."

Joanie allowed him to lead her out of the room without protest, but at the door she paused and, looking back at John, smiled shyly.

"I'll settle for one out of two," he said with a crooked smile.

"Frank is only disappointed because he likes to be dramatic. He probably saw himself introducing you to his friends and having them all cower. Then he could show his bravery by not being afraid," Melinda explained, attempting to take the sting out of Frank's unappreciative attitude. Then she flushed when she realized her explanation probably hadn't helped. "You did look a little fierce with all that hair," she added hesitantly.

"Has anyone ever told you that you have a great gift for taking one foot out of your mouth simply to make room for the other?" John asked dryly.

The flush on Melinda's cheeks darkened. "Many times."

Moving closer to her, a guardedness came over John's features. "Now for the really important question. How do *you* like my new look?"

Tracing the line of his lean, firm jaw with her fingertips, she took a moment to study his face. The nose that was slightly crooked from having been broken at least once— during barroom brawls, if she was to believe the rumors—was now more predominant, but it gave his face character. And there was a thin scar on his left cheek. Another souvenir from his rough past, no doubt. It added a dash of mystery. All in all, it was a face many women would find stimulating. "I have no complaints," she said.

Drawing her into his arms, he kissed the tip of her nose. "I'm glad to hear that."

"I'm glad you're glad," she returned, going up on tiptoe to kiss his freshly shaven cheek.

His hold on her tightened and her pulse quickened.

A quick knock on the door was followed immediately by Frank's entrance. "Joanie and I are really hungry," he said with impatience.

"So am I," John said, releasing Melinda and turning her toward the door. With a playful pat on her seat, he added in a low whisper, "And I can see I'm going to have to learn to lock doors when I want to satisfy aspects of my appetite that don't involve food."

"Go tell Joanie to come to the table, and the two of you can start making the toast," Melinda instructed Frank. Even before the last word was out, he was on his way downstairs. Turning back to John, she said apologetically, "I'm sorry we were interrupted. Privacy is a little hard to come by here."

"It's all right," he assured her. "The children are, after all, the number one priority."

Watching him as he moved away from her to find a shirt, her stomach twisted sharply. *I'd like to be his number one priority.* The thought filled her mind. Stop it! she ordered. You're only asking for trouble with wishes like that. Becoming mobile, she went downstairs to finish cooking breakfast.

Frank was unusually pensive while he and Joanie made the toast. This was a definite sign he had a concern on his mind. Melinda knew if she asked him, he would simply give her a whatever-gave-you-that-idea? look. So she waited. Eventually Frank's worries always surfaced. First they had to stew in his mind for a while.

When he glanced toward the door for the third time in as many minutes, it dawned on her that he was waiting for John. Now it was Melinda's turn to worry. She hadn't expected the children to accept John immediately, but she also hadn't expected them to present a strong resistance.

When John joined them at the table, Frank stopped what he had been telling Joanie in midsentence. Focusing his attention on his new uncle, there was a challenge in the set of his jaw. "Harriet says you have a home way up in the woods in Pennsylvania."

"Yes, I do," John answered levelly, showing no reaction to the hostile edge in the boy's voice.

"Are you going to make us move there?" The look on Frank's face suggested he would fight this idea to the death. "Tommy says that women always move into their husband's homes."

"Tommy doesn't know everything," Melinda said with a frown, wishing for the hundredth time she could muzzle Tommy. The child was always coming up with an opinion or suggestion that muddied the waters or caused trouble. She started to say so, but both John and Frank tossed her a glance that said they considered this a conversation between the two of them, and they wanted her to butt out. Deciding her interference wasn't going to help, she clamped her mouth shut.

"Are you going to move us?" Frank repeated the question.

"No." There was no patronizing undertone in John's voice. He addressed Frank as an equal with a legitimate concern. "I'm not going to move you to my home. Melinda has explained to me that your school and your friends are here. But I hope you'll want to visit my home once in a while. We can go hiking and fishing there."

"Visiting would be fine," Frank conceded, relief evident on his face as he turned and nodded to Joanie as if to say, I've taken care of the problem.

Joanie rewarded John with another shy smile and the mood at the breakfast table calmed noticeably.

Breathing a sigh of relief, Melinda asked Frank what he and his sister had been doing while she was gone and got a "Nothing much" in response.

Obviously anxious to get outside and tell Tommy they wouldn't be moving, both Joanie and Frank bolted down their food and asked to be excused.

"I'm sorry Frank seemed so hostile," Melinda apologized when she and John were alone. "It's just that they're still very insecure. Changes seem to be a threat to them."

"I understand."

She saw the shadow pass over his eyes and knew that he did. The urge to reach over and touch him was strong but she knew he would only draw away. Taking a final sip of coffee, she rose from the table and began clearing the plates.

Melinda was loading the dishwasher when a knock sounded on the front door. Certain it was Harriet come over to have a second look at John, she answered it with a smile, only to have the smile vanish when she opened the door.

"I see you're home. That was certainly a short honeymoon. Is he bored with you already?" Tall, slender, always dressed in expensive, well-cut clothes and with her gray hair always carefully coiffured, Adelle possessed an air of command. Her statements came out sounding like facts being delivered by a person in ultimate authority.

Melinda had learned to control her reactions to whatever Adelle might have to say. This morning, however, she had to admit that Adelle's cut felt particularly sharp. Still, she managed to keep her expression cool and indifferent. "What do you want?"

"I have come to see my grandchildren."

"Step-grandchildren," Melinda corrected. "Whom you ignored during the first four and five years of their lives."

"And now I'm trying to make up for lost time." Adelle's voice took on a honeyed tone. "These packages are getting heavy, and it's impolite to keep an elderly woman standing on the doorstep."

Melinda looked down at the two prettily wrapped gifts Adelle was carrying. "Why don't you give this up, Adelle? You're not going to get the children—or your hands on their trust fund."

Brushing past Melinda, Adelle stepped inside uninvited. "You do seem to have that trust on your mind," she mused. "Perhaps I should have it audited."

Melinda met the threat with icy confidence. "You will find that every cent is still there, plus interest."

Adelle smiled like a cat being offered a bowl of cream. "That's encouraging to hear." Then, looking past Melinda, her eyes narrowed speculatively. "Mr. Medwin, I presume?"

Turning, Melinda saw John coming toward them.

Suddenly Adelle was gushing defenseless charm. "Mr. Medwin, I know you believe marrying Melinda was heroic, but you're sadly mistaken. I love my grandchildren and want only what is best for them."

"You ignored them until you found out they had money of their own," Melinda pointed out curtly, her ego stinging from the way Adelle had pronounced the word *heroic* as if John had performed the ultimate sacrifice by marrying her.

Concentrating her attention on John, Adelle continued in a pleading voice. "I tried too hard to become a part of Judy's life. I wanted to be a real mother to her, not just a vague stepmother hovering in the shadows. But she resented me, and the harder I tried, the more alienated she became. I never realized how deeply jealous she was of her father's attentions until the night she left home. She made it clear she wanted nothing to do with him or me until I was out of his life. She wanted his complete attention or none at all. After she left home, she refused to even speak to either of us, and it was she who kept me away from my grandchildren. She refused to allow me to even speak to them."

Melinda tried to see behind the polite mask on John's face but couldn't. Had he believed Adelle? "That's a lie. It was you who kept Judy and her father apart. It was you who didn't want to share his attentions or his wealth."

Adelle dabbed at a small stream of tears trickling down her cheek. "My dear, your loyalty is commendable but misguided."

Melinda's hands balled into fists. Adelle was playing the part of the wounded party perfectly.

"You're going to allow me a few moments with my grandchildren, aren't you?" Adelle continued in a voice that suggested she greatly feared Melinda would deprive her of seeing Joanie and Frank.

Knowing that to continue any conversation with Adelle was futile, Melinda waved an arm toward the back of the house. "They're outside on the swing set."

"Thank you." Adelle exuded gratitude as she swept past Melinda and hurried toward the back door as if she was afraid Melinda might change her mind.

"I have never deprived her of seeing the children," Melinda said defensively, when she and John were alone. "No matter how much I've wanted to."

"Are you certain you haven't misjudged her?" he questioned in reasoning tones. "Maybe she honestly does regret the chasm she caused between herself and your sister-in-law. She's getting older and probably feels the need to have family around."

"The only need Adelle has ever felt is for money," Melinda seethed. Meeting John's gaze, she continued in a low hostile voice. "Do you think I would place myself in the humiliating position of asking a practically total stranger, a man with whom I have nothing in common, to marry me, if I thought there was the slightest chance I could have misjudged her motives?"

A shadow of anger passed across his face, then his mask was once again in place. "Put that way, no."

"I didn't mean that as an insult," Melinda apologized. Raking a hand through her hair, she added tightly, "Adelle makes me crazy. She's a consummate actress, and she's an expert at manipulating people." Melinda's gaze shifted toward the back of the house as shrieks of excitement issued from the backyard. "Like always bringing the children toys. It's like Christmas every time she comes to visit."

"I have noticed that while children enjoy the gifts Santa brings, very few want to sit on his lap and chat," John pointed out.

"I'll hold on to that thought." Melinda glanced toward him. Even though his expression was calm, she knew the anger was still there. He had to be regretting getting into this situation. And I can't blame him, she thought tiredly. Aloud she said, "I have dishes to wash," and escaped into the kitchen.

Chapter Seven

After putting the last dish in the dishwasher, Melinda went into the study. John was going to need a place to work, and she wanted to see if she could rearrange the room so they wouldn't be crowded. It was larger than most dens. In fact, it was larger than the living room. Originally it had been a screened-in porch, but her brother had had it glassed in and added heating units so it could be used year-round.

John was already there, standing in the

middle of the room surveying the furnishings when she entered.

Crossing to her wide-topped desk, she began to arrange the papers scattered over its surface. "I'll clean my clutter off the desk and you can have it."

"There are a couple of things we should get straight," he said, reaching the desk in two long strides and catching her hand to stop her. "The first is that you are going to need this desk. I'm not prepared to become a househusband with two small children to care for on a minute-by-minute basis. Therefore, you're to consider yourself, from this moment on, a permanently retired secretary. You'll spend your days caring for your—" he paused and corrected himself "—*our* niece and nephew, and concentrating on your writing. I'll take over paying the household expenses."

"Harriet will continue to watch the children while I work," she explained, shocked and a little embarrassed that he felt he would have to take over the entire fiscal responsibility for her and the children. "I never meant for you to take on our expenses."

"The children need to have you around. If you want to help with the household expenses, you've got talent. You can earn money with your writing." It was a command.

Melinda wasn't used to being bossed around. Even though she would love to be at home all the time with the children, no man was going to order her to be there! Her body tensed for battle. "Now, wait just one minute. I—"

"No," he cut her short. "So far you've set all the conditions for this marriage. It's only fair that I have a few things my way."

"That's true," she admitted. "But I didn't mean for this marriage to become a financial burden for you."

"It won't be a burden. My books have sold worldwide, and I've had very few personal expenses. The money I've earned has been invested rather than spent. I've a comfortable yearly income I'm sure we can subsist on."

"I've been on my own a long time." She persisted in her resistance, because she felt uncomfortable with the idea of being financially dependent on him, especially under the circumstances of their marriage.

"You have a book on the market now. You can contribute what monies you make to the household if you so desire," he said in a reasoning tone. His jaw hardened with purpose as he added, "But there will be no more temporary secretarial work for you. You've more important things to do with your time. You've got your career in writing and your niece and nephew to raise." Catching her by the chin, he tilted her face upward and placed a light kiss on her lips. "And I want a little wifely attention for myself from a woman who isn't exhausted from trying to be a mother, a secretary *and* a writer."

Melinda's heart pounded in her chest. "All right," she conceded, hating the weakness she felt for him that made her want to obey this last request with all the strength in her. "For now I'll consider myself retired from the temporary secretarial pool."

That point settled, John's gaze swung around the room. "If it won't bother you to have another person working in the same room, I'll buy a desk and filing cabinet and set up my space over there.'' He indicated a far corner of the room.

''That's fine with me,'' she agreed, suppressing frustrated anger. His touch had ignited a wanting in her while for him there had obviously been no reaction. She knew she was treading on dangerous ground, that she must be careful not to care too much. It's all hormonal, she assured herself with resolve.

''I'll need your car keys and the directions to the nearest bank,'' he was saying, interrupting her inner battle.

''They're on the table in the living room,'' she replied a little too coolly. Then in more moderate tones, she proceeded to give him a choice of banks, then directions to the one he chose.

A few minutes later, while she was sorting through the papers on her desk, she heard him leave the house. Immediately, she missed him. Furious with herself, she concentrated on sorting through the collection of junk mail that had arrived while she was gone.

"I'm amazed you actually managed to get a man as virile as John Medwin to marry you."

Swinging around, Melinda saw Adelle standing in the doorway of the den.

"I give him a month at the most before he becomes bored out of his mind in this Mary Poppins household and goes berserk." Having made this pronouncement, Adelle smiled sweetly and, with a wave of her hand, left.

"Me, too," Melinda admitted in a self-directed whisper as she heard the front door opening and closing again.

"You, too, what?" Frank asked, entering the room to show her his new toy.

"I was having a private conversation with myself," she replied, adding, "And it's impolite to eavesdrop." Then her expression softened measurably as she saw Joanie peeking around the door with a worried look on her face. "Is something wrong?" she asked, going over and kneeling in front of the little girl.

"No." Joanie's lips clamped shut and she shook her head.

"You know you can tell me anything," Melinda coaxed gently.

"This is Ruff." Joanie held up the stuffed puppy Adelle had brought her. "He doesn't think he's going to like Uncle John."

The urge to kill Adelle was strong. Melinda was certain the woman had done what she could do to turn the child against John. "I'm sure he'll like him once he gets to know him. Uncle John is a very nice man. You know I wouldn't bring anyone into this house who wasn't nice, don't you?"

"I suppose," Joanie conceded. But there was a dubiousness in her voice that suggested she wasn't totally convinced.

Knowing time was the only real solution to this problem, Melinda allowed the subject to drop and spent a few minutes admiring Ruff and the plane that transformed into a robot that had been Frank's gift. Then, going upstairs, she began rearranging closets and drawers and unpacking John's clothing.

"I just can't believe it."

Melinda gave a small gasp of surprise, then spun around to find Harriet standing in the doorway of the bedroom.

"Didn't mean to startle you," the older woman apologized, entering and seating herself on the edge of the bed. "I saw John and Adelle leave, so I thought I would pop over for a few private words. The children answered the door before I even had a chance to knock and told me you were up here." Picking up one of John's shirts, she held it up in front of her as if checking it for size and said again, "I just can't believe it."

Scowling darkly, Melinda turned to face her. "I wish people would quit being so *amazed* that John Medwin married me. I feel like one of the ugly stepsisters in Cinderella who unexpectedly ends up with the prince."

"I didn't mean it that way." Getting up from the bed, Harriet gave Melinda a motherly hug. "I'm just so happy for you. I was worried when you left. I know we both agreed that an arranged marriage in this day and age had as good a chance as any other of surviving, but you seemed anxious about facing John Medwin and I was concerned."

Picking up one of John's sweaters, Melinda frowned down at it. "I didn't mean to snap at you," she apologized. "I'm just not so certain this marriage was such a good idea."

"He hasn't mistreated you, has he?" Harriet seemed ready to do battle with John if he had.

"No." A self-conscious flush darkened Melinda's cheeks. "He's been very...nice. It's just that we married because of the children and because he wants heirs of his own. There's no deep emotional commitment and I'm not sure how long it will last."

"Do you want it to last?" Harriet questioned.

"If he wants it to," Melinda answered honestly.

Harriet gave her another hug. "Then I wish you the best. Like I said last night, you've always been able to do anything you set your mind to."

But no one can will another person to love her, Melinda thought bitterly, then was furious with herself for even thinking of love and John in the same moment. Thoughts like that could only lead to pain and disillusionment.

The front door opened and closed. For a moment, Melinda wondered if one or both of the children had gone out without telling her, then she heard Frank describing how to transform his newest toy and knew that John was back.

"Nice to see you again," he greeted Harriet as she and Melinda descended the stairs.

Harriet frowned in mild confusion. 'You've shaved off your beard—or was I dreaming last night?'

"He shaved it off because it scared Joanie," Frank answered, glancing toward his sister with impatience, as if he'd determined John was not a danger and was angry with her for not believing him.

Joanie had been peeking around the kitchen door at her brother and John. With Melinda and Harriet's arrival, she edged into the hall and over to stand against Melinda.

The worried look she'd had earlier was even more pronounced. "What's wrong?" Embarrassed that Joanie was acting as if John might eat her at any moment, Melinda knelt down in front of the child. "I told you that you have nothing to be afraid of."

"She overheard Grandma Adelle say Uncle John would get bored out of his mind in a month and go berserk and she's worried about what he'll do to us," Frank blurted out when Joanie steadfastly refused to speak. "She thinks he might start wrecking things and hurting people."

"And I think you've been watching too much television." Melinda scowled, her embarrassment at Joanie's attitude toward John deepening further. She couldn't blame him if he greeted this harsh judgement of his character with anger. But when she glanced toward him, she saw understanding in his eyes.

"I never break things when I go berserk. I go looking for an ice-cream shop and buy the most gigantic sundae they have and eat until I think I'm going to burst," he said matter-of-factly. Then, with an encouraging smile, he asked, "You wouldn't happen to know of a place where I could get a big sundae, would you? Just in case."

"Custards Galore," Joanie answered hesitantly.

"I don't suppose you and Frank would like to direct me there so I can get a look at the place and try out their ice cream?" he suggested.

Joanie maintained a death grip on Melinda's hand. "Aunt Melinda should go, too. She knows the way."

"Of course she'll go," John agreed.

Melinda started to point out that the children hadn't had lunch, then decided against it. Their getting to know and like John was more important than one ruined meal.

But as if he could read her mind, he added, "We'll stop and have a hamburger first, though. Ice cream needs something to sit on."

"And french fries?" Frank asked, reaching up and taking the man's hand.

"Anything you want," John assured him. Then, turning toward Harriet, he said, "You're welcome to come along, too."

"No, I've got a bit of knitting I need to get done," she replied. "But thank you for the invite." Giving Melinda a final hug, she added in a whisper, "You all make a beautiful family group."

On the surface we do, Melinda corrected mentally, determined to keep the situation in perspective.

It was later that evening when a new worry began to torment her. John was sitting in the middle of the playroom floor. Frank was seated beside him demonstrating how to transform a variety of his toys from cars, boats, planes and other gadgets into robots. Watching the child's face, Melinda could see he was developing an attachment to his new uncle. Even Joanie seemed fascinated by John. She'd always been a shy child and her imagined fears had produced a temporary barrier. But the afternoon had gone exceptionally well. After the lunch and ice cream, John had taken them to the park. By the end of the day, Joanie's fear had faded dramatically. Now she sat a little to one side of John, watching her brother but mostly watching John, this time with curiosity and interest.

Melinda wanted the children to like John, but now she found herself worrying about them becoming too close to him. She couldn't shake her fear that this marriage wasn't going to be permanent, and Joanie and Frank didn't need another loss in their lives. She felt trapped between a rock and a hard place.

You've got to think positively. You've got to believe you can hold it together, she commanded herself. But it wasn't easy. And everyone's amazement that John had actually married her in the first place haunted her. Maybe that's because I'm so amazed myself, she admitted, and forcing her worries to the back of her mind, she joined the others on the floor.

But a week and a half later, her fears about the stability of the marriage were sharply reawakened. Her decision to ask John to marry her had been a spur-of-the-moment act of desperation, and because of that, she'd taken no precautions against getting pregnant. John hadn't either, which had seemed natural since he'd mentioned he wanted a family as one of his reasons for agreeing to this marriage. For her part, Melinda had felt ambivalent when it became evident earlier in the day that she wasn't pregnant yet. One side of her wanted very much to give John a child, while a more practical side insisted she should wait until their marriage was more secure. All day long the battle raged within her. Finally, her less practical side won and she decided to let nature take its course.

But John had other ideas.

"Since it's now obvious you're not pregnant," he said, lying down beside her, "I've been thinking it would be best if we begin practicing some sort of birth control. I think the four of us need time to get used to one another before we add a fifth."

She knew he was being reasonable and practical. But she couldn't help also seeing this as a sign he was having serious second thoughts about their marriage. "Of course," she agreed with forced nonchalance, making a mental note to contact her lawyer the next day and find out how long the marriage would need to last to satisfy Judge Craras that they had tried. Then, because she still had her pride, she heard herself adding, "Having children was one of your gratuities in this marriage."

Levering himself up so he could look down into her face, he glared at her angrily. "Children are not gratuities. They are human beings who need to be wanted by both parents."

"I didn't mean it that way," she defended stiffly. "I would want any child I gave birth to."

"No matter who the father was," he finished coldly.

Her jaw tightened. "The father would matter to me." Pride again overpowered prudence as she added curtly, "And I would want him to be someone who wanted me to have his children."

"Now wait a minute." Catching her before she could turn her back on him, he looked hard into her face. "If you got the impression that I don't want you to bear my children, you're wrong. I do want us, you and me, to have children. I simply thought it would be a good idea to give ourselves and Joanie and Frank a little time to adjust to our current situation before making an addition."

Melinda's stomach knotted. She had overreacted and made a fool of herself again. Even worse, she'd come very close to letting him see how much his wanting to wait had hurt. "I get very emotional at this time of the month. Could we just forget the last part of this conversation took place?" she requested through clenched teeth.

"I've heard that can happen to women," he said, continuing to study her narrowly. "Just so we understand one another, I do want us to have children."

The desire to have his children was so strong she was afraid he might read it in her eyes. Nodding her understanding, she said, "I'm really tired."

Releasing her, he lay back down, and in a few minutes his regular breathing told her he was asleep. She stared at the ceiling and her mouth formed a hard, straight line. She didn't want to care so much.

You've fallen in love with him, her inner voice accused. *Now you're in real trouble.*

Chapter Eight

During the next few days, life settled into a workable routine. Frank became John's shadow and even Joanie tagged along behind her new uncle. One afternoon, arriving home from doing the grocery shopping, Melinda had found them playing quietly on the floor in the middle of the den with John pounding away at his typewriter in the corner. Normally they preferred being out in the backyard or down in the playroom. She'd told them not to disturb John while he was working, but children will be children. She guessed they'd gotten into a squabble and he'd been forced to allow them to play in the den to keep an eye on them. Monitoring the children while he worked was her job, she reminded herself curtly, angry with herself for not asking Harriet to watch them while she was out. Apologizing to him, she'd started to run them out but he'd stopped her. "They don't bother me," he assured her. "Let them stay." From then on, at least a part of Frank and Joanie's day was spent in the den.

More and more, Melinda would find herself worrying about how the children would react if John were to vanish from their lives as quickly as he had entered them. Then, telling herself that worry wasn't going to do any good, she'd force it aside. But it lingered in the back of her mind, nagging at her. And it wasn't just Joanie and Frank she was worried about. She didn't want to face the possible reality of his leaving, either.

It was on a Friday afternoon, about three weeks after Melinda and John had married, when Fletcher Godwin came to call. Later Melinda wished she'd warned John about

Fletcher, but Fletcher was not an easy person to explain until one had some firsthand experience. And, as usual, he came without warning. John answered the door to find the tall, blond man in his early thirties—with decidedly handsome features and dressed like Sherlock Holmes—standing on the doorstep.

"I've come to see the dark-eyed sorceress Melinda about our murder," Fletcher announced dramatically, taking a puff on the large-bowled meerschaum pipe he was holding in the side of his mouth.

Regarding him suspiciously as if he was afraid the man might be slightly deranged, John led Fletcher into the den. "You have a caller," he said, stepping aside to allow Fletcher to enter ahead of him.

"Melinda, you look radiant." Crossing to her desk, Fletcher performed a deep bow and, taking her right hand in his, placed a light kiss on its back. Continuing to maintain the manner of the famous detective, he released her right hand and captured her left. "My sources tell me changes have taken place in your life since last we met." Regret spread across his face. "'Tis true. You have married." Releasing her hand, he turned to face John dourly. "And if my sources continue to be correct, you must be John Medwin. Fletcher Godwin at your service, sir." Fletcher paused to perform a deep bow. When he straightened, his manner was threatening. "You had best prove to be a good husband to this woman or you shall have me to answer to."

Covering a flush of embarrassment, Melinda frowned indulgently. "Fletcher, really."

His dourness vanishing, he turned back toward her. "You don't like my Sherlock-Holmes-being-protective-toward-the-fair-maiden act?" he said with mock despair, adding with a mischievous grin, "I've been rehearsing for a PBS filming of *Hound of the Baskervilles* all day. Thought you might enjoy seeing me in character."

"You're always in character," she tossed back, forcing a nonchalance into her voice. It was silly to overreact to Fletcher.

"Is he safe to have around?" John asked dryly.

"Just barely," she answered, rewarding Fletcher with a humoring smile.

Doffing the hat and gloves, Fletcher offered John his hand. "It's a pleasure to meet you. I've read all your books. Hope to star as Nicolus Blade on the screen someday."

The children entered the room as John accepted the handshake.

"Got a hug for ole Uncle Fletcher?" Fletcher asked, squatting down to their level.

With a chorus of giggles, both children threw their arms around his neck. He returned their hug and, after giving each a kiss on the cheek, produced two gigantic lollipops.

"Take them down to the playroom to eat," Melinda instructed in response to the question in their eyes as they glanced toward her. "And remember your manners."

Joanie rewarded Fletcher with an even broader smile. "Thank you."

"Yeah, thanks." Frank echoed the sentiment, adding as he walked toward the door, "The armor was neater."

"The last time Fletcher came, he'd been rehearsing for Camelot and came dressed in his chain mail and leg armor," Melinda explained when John glanced toward her questioningly. Then, turning her attention to Fletcher, she said solicitously, "Aren't you hot in that suit coat and vest? The last time I checked outside, it was still the middle of summer and the temperature was over ninety."

"We actors must suffer for our trade," he replied with exaggerated self-sacrifice. "However, since I'm not on stage at the moment..."

"I always think of you as being on stage at any given moment," Melinda mused playfully.

"I've heard that accusation before," he muttered, tossing the hat and gloves onto the daybed and unbuttoning the suit coat. "However, my dark-eyed beauty, you, I am willing to forgive." Sending the suit coat and vest to join the hat and gloves, he changed his demeanor once again. Curling an imaginary handlebar mustache between his fingers, he said in a villainous tone, "And now to business. We have need to discuss *the murder.*"

Again, Melinda felt she needed to offer John some sort of explanation. "I've written a participation murder play for Fletcher and his troupe to perform at Fort Delaware as a fund-raiser for the fort."

Fletcher waved his arm in the manner of a barker at a sideshow. "For a donation of one hundred and fifty dollars apiece, Wilmington society will be given an evening of wine, food and entertainment."

Crossing his arms in front of him and leaning against the doorjamb, John regarded the actor dubiously. The expression on his face suggested he wouldn't be surprised if Fletcher meant to commit a real murder. "What exactly is a participation murder play?"

Fletcher's eyes glowed with enthusiasm. "The guests are given a set-up story. In this case, since the fort's greatest claim to fame— or I suppose I should say infamy—is that it was the Union forces' largest prisoner-of-war camp during the War Between the States, Melinda has devised a plot around that. Following the Battle of Gettysburg, all the Confederate prisoners captured there were brought to the fort to join a few thousand already housed on the island. That brought the number up to over twelve thousand. They couldn't all be housed in the fort, so most were placed in wooden barracks outside the walls. But the generals and higher-ranking officers, a few very important Confederate political prisoners and the real troublemakers were housed inside the fort.

"According to Melinda's scenario, one of the prisoners housed inside the fort hid some very incriminating documents. Those documents have been recently discovered and are to be read following the dinner we'll be serving at the fort. For various reasons, members of the cast will want to get their hands on them. Some are playing family members who want to destroy them before an ancestor is labeled a traitor. Others want to steal the documents and sell them to the highest bidder. All in all, there will be two murders and one attempted murder. During the evening the actors will mingle among the guests dropping hints, and having a few trysting scenes. The trick is that the guests won't know who the actors are. They'll have to sort out what's happening and who's actually involved. Then, as the murders begin to take place, I will appear in the guise of Detective Peeps, and the guests will be given a chance to help me unravel the plot."

Comprehension dawned on John's face. "I've heard that sort of thing has become a fad."

"And a very profitable one," Fletcher assured him. Then, turning his attention to Melinda, he said, "I've made a few notes on your script. I was hoping we could go over them. The Event is going to take place in five weeks, and I want to begin casting the parts next week."

Not wanting to interfere with John's work, Melinda motioned toward the door. "We can go over them in the living room."

For the next hour and a half she and Fletcher went over the script, line by line. A few new quips came to mind and were added. A few lines he thought were too cliché were removed.

"I still think you and I should go to the fort and walk our way through this over the weekend. I want to make certain we haven't missed anything," he said when they were finally finished.

"Fine," she agreed, rising and massaging her lower back muscles. They had been sitting on the couch with her script spread out on the coffee table, and leaning forward to make notations was threatening to send the muscles into spasms. Next time, she promised herself, they would use the dining room table.

Rising to stand behind her, Fletcher began massaging her shoulders. Abruptly, as if reaching a decision, he turned her around to face him. "You could've come to me if you felt you needed a husband."

Startled, Melinda stared at him in disbelief. She had grown used to Fletcher saying the unexpected. But linking his name and *husband* in the same sentence was a shock.

"You don't have to play innocent with me," he continued gruffly. "I know the whole story. I was here visiting with Harriet and the kids when Adelle came over and found out about your marriage. She said a lot of things. Luckily most were out of earshot of the kids. When she left, I questioned

Harriet. She's not a very good liar. I know you married John Medwin in an act of desperation to keep Joanie and Frank.''

"If you're really my friend, you'll never repeat that to anyone," she choked out in a panic.

"I'd never place you in danger of losing the children," he assured her. "I just wish you had come to me. I know I've never espoused the virtues of fatherhood and when you became guardian of your niece and nephew I made a few disparaging cracks about instant parenthood, but I've always cared for you. I would've married you.''

Melinda looked up into the wistful blue eyes. Fletcher's parents had owned the house across the street, and she'd known him all her life. And she also knew, as certainly as she knew her own name, he was playing a role. He was always playing roles. That was his existence. Each time he adopted a new role, he convinced himself for the time being that he was sincere. But after a while he would tire of what he termed "a life rut," and move on to new interests. That he was her friend and would attempt to do anything he could to help her, she didn't doubt. That he could sustain any kind of long-term commitment, she did doubt. "You've tried living with three different women," she pointed out. "Each time, within six months, you began suffering pangs of confinement. Marriage would be claustrophobic to you."

"You're wrong." Cupping her face in his hands, he placed a light kiss on her lips. "With you it would be different. You understand me. With you I feel a bond."

"It's friendship, not love," she assured him. A prickling sensation on the back of her neck caused her to glance toward the door.

John was standing there watching them, his gaze narrowed dangerously. "I came to ask if either of you wanted a cold drink. It appears you may need a cold shower instead."

"That's unfair and uncalled for," Melinda snapped.

Moving in front of her as if to shield her with his body, Fletcher met John's gaze levelly. "I'd never try to seduce Melinda. I respect her too much. I merely wanted her to know that if this marriage didn't work out and she felt the need for a new husband, I'm available.''

"You really know how to improve a situation," Melinda muttered, stepping out from behind him. "I think it would be best if you leave, Fletcher."

"Perhaps," he agreed, seeing John's gaze darkening further. Still, he refused to be entirely intimidated. Pausing as he passed John, he said, "I hope you realize how lucky you are, Medwin."

"One man's luck is another man's poison," John muttered under his breath as Fletcher continued toward the den to collect his discarded clothing.

Fletcher was out of earshot but Melinda wasn't. "Poison!" she seethed, anger hiding the hurt.

"I didn't mean that," John apologized gruffly. "I'm still in shock from finding my wife in another man's arms."

"I wasn't in his arms," she corrected, trying to convince herself he meant the apology but not entirely succeeding.

"He was kissing you and offering himself to you," he pointed out.

"You don't understand Fletcher," she defended tightly. "He's just role-playing."

The scowl on John's face deepened. "Role-playing?"

"Fletcher is a born actor," she elaborated, trying to keep her voice in a reasoning mode. But the sting of being referred to as "poison" was still strong, and her tone was frosty. "Today he's playing the faithful suitor who would gladly die for me. And he has convinced himself he really feels that way. But by next week, he'll have found a new interest. He's like a little boy who'll never grow up."

"I'd grow up for you, Melinda," Fletcher vowed.

Glancing down the hall, Melinda saw him approaching them.

Coming to a halt beside John, Fletcher's gaze riveted on him. "You'd better keep that in mind, Medwin. I'm here for her if she ever needs me." Having made this pronouncement, he continued to the front door. But with his hand on the knob, he turned back.

"I'll pick you up at ten tomorrow, Melinda," he added, and was gone before she could make any utterance in response.

John's jaw twitched in an outward sign of the struggle he was having controlling his temper. Folding his arms in front of him, he stared at her as if trying to read her soul. "I want to know what's going on between you and Fletcher."

"Nothing!" She met his hostility with an anger of her own. "You just have to learn to understand Fletcher and not take anything he says too seriously. He's like a child playing at the dramatic."

"What did he mean when he said he'd be picking you up at ten tomorrow?" he demanded.

Momentarily she was tempted to tell him it wasn't any of his business. But prudence intervened. "It's strictly business. We have to go to the fort tomorrow and walk through the murder," she answered icily.

"I was under the impression you needed *me* to marry you—to save your reputation and allow you to keep the children," John observed dryly.

Melinda's back stiffened. "If you're implying I had a choice between you and Fletcher and chose you just to make your life miserable, you're mistaken. Being single would give me more of a chance with Judge Craras than being married to Fletcher."

"What I was attempting to point out," he said with a strong edge of sarcasm, "is that Adelle is looking for gossip to use against you. Going to the fort with Fletcher, especially in his present ardent mood, could lead to a scandal."

Angry with herself for misinterpreting his remark, but even more angry with him for not denying her description of his present existence as miserable, she said cuttingly, "I'll take the children along."

"I think it would be best if all of us went." It was a command.

He didn't believe what she had said about Fletcher. He didn't trust her! That was the worst cut of all. The need to escape from this confrontation before she said something she might regret was essential. "Suit yourself," she muttered, stalking out of the room and down the hall. In the kitchen she discovered her hands were shaking. Why should he trust you? she chided acidly. Trust comes with friendship and love. All the two of us have is a mutual concern for the children and a strong lust for each other's bodies.

Trying not to dwell on how flimsy her marriage was, she went grocery shopping. She returned home to find Philip Ross's car parked in front of her house. "When it rains, it pours," she muttered grimly, guessing why Philip had come.

John came out to meet her. Taking the bag of groceries from her, he said coolly, "Your lawyer is here. He's been polite but very closemouthed. If his visit has something to do with Adelle, I think I should be included."

She saw the impatient anger in his eyes and behind that, the distrust. She didn't like lying. Besides, what Philip had to say would be of interest to John. "He's probably here to give me the answer to the question I asked him several days ago," she said, forcing her voice to sound businesslike. "After we had the discussion about waiting to have children, I thought it would be prudent . . ." She paused momentarily, wanting to choose her words carefully. "It occurred to me our marriage was no more stable than any other. Therefore, there was the chance we might not be able to hold it together even for the sake of the children." *A big chance,* she added mentally, considering what had already passed between them today. "Anyway, I asked Philip how long the marriage would have to last to satisfy Judge Craras that we had tried."

For a moment the anger in John's eyes darkened, then his expression became closed. "A very practical question," he said, and continued into the house with the grocery bags.

"Very practical," she muttered, following him. But not one she wanted to ask. As much as she hated to admit it, she dreaded the thought of losing John. But she cared too much to hold him against his will.

"I decided it would be best to come by to speak to you in the privacy of your home," Philip said, rising to greet her when she entered the living room. "Even in a lawyer's office we can never fully ensure against gossips."

"I think it would be best if we discussed this in the den," she suggested. "That room has a door we can close so the children can't accidentally overhear what we discuss."

Nodding his agreement, Philip followed her down the hall. "I've looked into this matter personally," he said as they entered the den. His manner became that of a father deeply concerned about a child's behavior. "I did offer the idea of this marriage as a possible solution. As your lawyer, it was my duty to outline all of the possibilities. But marriage to John Medwin was, as I pointed out, a drastic solution and one to be acted on only when everything else failed."

"It was my opinion that everything else was going to fail," she replied in her defense.

"Perhaps," he admitted. "Either way, what's done is done, and we must make the best of it."

"Make the best of what?" John questioned coldly. He had stopped in the kitchen to put the bags of groceries on the counter and had entered the den at the end of Philip's sentence.

"I thought he should be included," Melinda said, answering the question in Philip's glance as his gaze swung from her to John and back to her. "After all, this does involve him."

Philip rewarded Melinda's wish with an approving nod. "I'm pleased you're able to join us." He addressed John. Then, with the practice of one who has trained himself to control any given situation, he seated himself and waved a hand to indicate he wanted Melinda and John to be seated also.

Melinda chose the daybed, but John, as if he sensed a confrontation, did not seat himself beside her. Instead, he pulled his desk chair over, and she could almost feel a new barrier being built between them.

"Your question was—" Philip addressed Melinda in a professional voice "—should this marriage not work out, how long must it be sustained to satisfy Judge Craras that you tried?"

Melinda glanced toward John, but his expression remained shuttered.

"I've checked into this question carefully," Philip continued, his frown deepening as he followed Melinda's glance and also found John's face unreadable. "And I have concluded that for you to satisfy Judge Craras you have tried, five years together will be necessary. If the two of you discover you are incompatible, I know this can seem like a long time, but it will pass. I'm afraid there's no way out that won't greatly weaken Melinda's chances of keeping the children."

"Thank you for looking into the matter," Melinda said, breaking the silence that fell over the room as Philip paused for their comments.

"Yes, thank you," John added in a bland voice, giving no evidence of how he felt about the conversation.

Rising, Philip extended his hand toward John. "Glad I had this opportunity to meet you," he said, studying the face in front of him as if to discover some hint of what was going on in John's mind. The fact that he could read nothing seemed to make him uneasy. Turning to Melinda, he said, "Will you walk an old man to his car?"

It was more than a request. "Of course." For a moment, she saw anger flash from be-

hind John's calm facade and was tempted to
tell Philip that whatever else he had to say to
her could be said in front of John. But she
held her tongue. She trusted Philip, and if he
had something he wanted to say to her pri-
vately, she should allow him that privilege.
Slipping her arm through Philip's, she
walked with him out of the house.

"I've been worried about you ever since
your phone call," he said, patting in a fatherly manner her hand tucked around his
arm. "At that time, you assured me your
husband was not mistreating you. But another reason for me to come by your home
was that I wanted to meet him and reassure
myself you were speaking the truth." They
had reached Philip's car and he looked down
at her like a Dutch uncle, the concern on his
face deepening. "The problem is, I'm not
reassured. John Medwin is an unreadable
man, and I'm not used to that. It makes me
suspicious."

"He's guarded," she admitted. "But he's
been very good to me, and the children like
him," Melinda continued, defending John
firmly. "If anyone is at fault in this mar-

riage, it's me. He married me because he was
an abandoned child and could sympathize
with Joanie and Frank's situation. But I'm
afraid five years is going to seem like a very
long time to him once the heroic glow of his
gesture begins to wear off.''

Philip gave her hand an encouraging
squeeze. ''You're a sweet, lovely woman.
Spending five years of his life with you
shouldn't be so difficult.''

She was tempted to point out that John
had always had his pick of the loveliest and
most exciting females. But the words tasted
sour on her tongue and she merely thanked
Philip once again for coming and said
goodbye.

Entering the kitchen, she found John
cleaning up a container of melting ice cream
that had been at the bottom of the bag of
groceries he'd left sitting on the table. ''Are
you going to tell me what else your lawyer
had to say to you?'' he questioned caustically.

The look on his face dared her not to. ''He
wanted to reassure himself you weren't mistreating me. I told him you were good to me

and the children liked you," she replied levelly.

"But you're still anxious to see this marriage end," he added.

Melinda's jaw tightened. "You were the one who made it clear you weren't certain this marriage would work. You were the one who suggested having children was a bit premature. I simply thought it would be prudent to find out how long we had to remain together so all of this won't have been in vain."

Sarcasm etched itself into his features. "I see. It's only my feelings that prompted your questions about the necessary duration of our marriage. As far as you're concerned, you'd be happy for it to continue forever."

A yes almost slipped out, but pride held it back. "I didn't want you to feel you were trapped for life once the Arthurian heroics of your gesture began to wear off," she replied coolly.

"I suppose I should be grateful that you're so concerned about *me* feeling trapped," he sneered, and stalked out of the house.

She was tempted to run after him, but what would she say? She certainly couldn't confess her real feelings for him. Tears of frustration burned at the back of her eyes. Refusing to give in to them, she finished cleaning up the ice cream and put away the rest of the groceries.

Chapter Nine

John said very little during dinner. He spent
the evening playing with the children, and
when they went to bed, he went into the den
and began typing. Melinda refused to make
the first move toward peace. She'd behaved
in a reasonable and open manner. A few
words weren't going to change the fact that
he didn't trust her.

Depressed and tired, she went to bed. But
sleep didn't come easily. She tossed and
turned and finally admitted to herself that
she was waiting for John. But by two in the

morning he still hadn't come to bed and she finally fell into a restless sleep.

When she awoke the next morning, she discovered she was still alone. A sad aching filled her. Gently, she ran her hand over his pillow. A few lazy tears slid from the corners of her eyes. Furious with herself for missing him so much, she jerked her hand back and bolted from the bed.

Downstairs she found him asleep on the daybed in the den. He'd stripped to his jeans, and there was a notepad and pencil on the floor beside him. She tried telling herself he hadn't come up to bed because he'd fallen asleep while he was working. But she knew it was a lie. The lights had been turned out. Even in sleep he looked angry, and suddenly five years seemed like an eternity.

Not wanting to wake him, she kept the children quiet when they got up. All the time she was feeding them breakfast, she debated waking John. The truth was, she finally admitted, she didn't want another confrontation. Too much had been said already. Cleaning up the dishes, she glanced at the clock. It was already ten to ten. She'd called

Fletcher and told him they would meet him at the ferry at eleven and it was only prudent to give herself forty-five minutes for the drive to Delaware City. The children were upstairs dressing. She had to make a decision about waking John.

"Isn't Uncle John going to the fort with us?" Frank asked, appearing suddenly in the kitchen doorway.

Startled by the intrusion into her mental battle, Melinda almost dropped the plate she was drying. "I really don't know if I should wake—" she answered, turning to face the child only to have the last of the sentence die as she met John's cold gaze.

His bare feet had allowed him to come up behind the boy undetected. Raking a hand through his hair to comb it out of his face, he wore a grim look. "I wouldn't miss this for the world."

"Uncle John!" Frank whirled around, a broad smile splitting his face. "You'll love it. They have dungeons!"

"A perfect setting for your aunt," John muttered, his gaze remaining steadily on Melinda. Then, abruptly turning toward the stairs, he said briskly, "I'd better shave if we're going to be on time. Wouldn't want to keep Fletcher waiting."

"I'll come watch." Frank started to scurry up the stairs after him.

"No!" Melinda moved swiftly, catching the child's arm before his foot hit the first step. "You go downstairs and watch cartoons with your sister."

"He doesn't mind if I watch," Frank protested.

"Go!" Melinda ordered, pointing toward the playroom. Her voice held a threat of punishment if he disobeyed, and with an unhappy shrug, Frank did as he was told.

Climbing the stairs, Melinda paused at the door of the bedroom and counted to ten to regain control. Then, taking a final deep breath, she entered the room. John was standing in front of the sink in the adjoining bathroom smearing shaving cream over his face. Coming to a halt in the doorway of the bathroom, she faced him levelly. "I don't feel trapped. I know you won't believe me but I really was thinking of you. You gave up a great deal and gained very little. I

gave up very little and gained a great deal.''
Then, turning on her heel, she stalked out of
the bedroom.

The drive to Delaware City seemed inter-
minable. John said little, merely responding, when required, to Frank and Joanie's
constant chatter. Melinda said nothing. The
more her mind dwelt on John's behavior
during the past days, the more convinced she
became he was beginning to feel trapped.
There had been an underlying uneasiness
about him. Tersely she recalled the evening
when all four of them had been sitting
around the television, eating popcorn and
laughing through a Muppet movie. John had
suddenly left and gone for a walk. He'd said
he suddenly felt the need to exercise but now
she pictured him feeling like the world was
closing in on him. Of course he wouldn't
want to admit that, so he was accusing her of
wanting out instead.

To make matters worse, Fletcher was still
playing the I-want-to-be-your-hero role
when they met at the wharf. He was gregar-
ious with the children while being con-

stantly at Melinda's side, ready to respond to her slightest whim.

The fort was not a well-known tourist attraction. Because very little money was allotted for its upkeep, it remained in a tattered condition—but that was part of its charm. The day was overcast and Melinda wasn't surprised to discover they were to be the only passengers on the ferry. Boarding for the short trip to Pea Patch Island, she sat down along the rail. Fletcher sat down next to her. John, however, chose to sit on the long row of seats in the center of the boat with the children on either side of him. She caught the glint of steel in his eyes when Fletcher laid his arm along the rail behind her, and she was momentarily tempted to act as if she was enjoying Fletcher's attentions. But she wasn't enjoying this one little bit and to pretend she was would only worsen an already strained relationship. So instead she sat stiffly, reacting to everything Fletcher said and did in a purely businesslike manner.

When the boat docked, each child claimed one of John's hands. Joanie was practically dancing as they made their way down the long pier to the waiting jitney that would carry them through the foxtail-filled marsh to the fort.

"The children really seem to be taken in by him," Fletcher remarked in a lowered voice in Melinda's ear as they followed several paces behind. His tone suggested that John's behavior toward the children was a sham.

Without reservation, Melinda came to John's defense. "He cares a great deal about them and they know it. Children can sense that sort of thing."

"I did read somewhere that he had an unfortunate childhood," Fletcher mused. "I suppose he feels a bond." Then, his voice becoming dramatically protective, he asked, "But what about you? Are you happy with him?"

This time she had to force the sincerity into her voice. "Yes, I'm happy."

The protectiveness in Fletcher's manner became even more pronounced. "Your happiness means a great deal to me. If he should ever disappoint you in any way, he'll have me to answer to."

Melinda imagined Fletcher seeing himself in a Dirty Harry style role straightening out John. She was definitely going to have to talk to him before his dramatics caused the rift between her and John to widen even more.

As on the ferry, John sat between the children on the jitney. Emerging into the small park surrounding the fort, the tractor-pulled conveyance came to a halt in front of the combination footbridge and drawbridge spanning the thirty-foot moat surrounding the fort. Climbing down, Frank and Joanie again each claimed one of John's hands and began pulling him toward the sally port.

"We'll go to the very top first," Frank said, outlining the tour he had planned. "Then we'll come down behind where the big guns used to be and back through the dungeons."

"Be certain you hold John's hands on the ramparts," Melinda instructed, her gaze darting dubiously to the open level three stories above them. To John she added with a plea in her voice, "It's very uneven up there. It was built up with dirt and at one time even trees grew up there. The lay of the land is rough and there's not much of a railing."

"I won't allow any harm to come to the children," he assured her.

His words felt like a double-edged sword twisting inside her. But she managed a thank-you smile. "You two do whatever John says," she called after the trio as the children began pulling John toward the spiral granite staircase at the far side of the parade grounds.

"I think we should start in the rooms where the important Confederate prisoners were quartered," Fletcher said, pulling her attention back to him. Placing his hand on the small of her back, he gave her a gentle nudge toward a narrow staircase at the side of the sally port.

Worriedly, she glanced back toward John and the children now disappearing into the stairwell. Then she shrugged. The one thing she didn't need to worry about was John taking good care of Frank and Joanie. And this would give her a chance to have a private, firm talk with Fletcher.

Mounting the stairs, she entered the second level. Inside the main prisoners' room, her gaze traveled around the walls. Above and to the side of the fireplace, the plaster had fallen away, exposing the bare brick. The deep windowsills and the plank wood floor were covered with a thick layer of dust. "You're going to have to hire a cleaning crew," she said, drawing a circle with the toe of her shoe in the dust. "People who pay a hundred and fifty dollars for a ticket are going to want their antique cleaned up a bit. They'll get enough of this kind of atmosphere in the back quarters and dungeons."

"I'm much more practical than you give me credit for," Fletcher chided her with mock reprimand. "I've already taken care of that. The entire route will be swept and despiderwebbed."

Since they'd ridden over on the first ferry, there were no other tourists at the fort. From experience, Melinda knew the two rangers assigned to the fort would most likely remain in the parade area or their offices. Therefore, she decided, this was the perfect time to have her private chat with Fletcher. "I have a favor to ask you," she said.

"Anything," he pledged, coming to stand in front of her and taking her hands in his.

"I don't need a protector," she said with slow deliberation to place emphasis on what she had to say. "What I need is someone who'll be a good friend to both me and John."

Fletcher squeezed her hands. "You know I'd do anything for you."

"Then you'll start behaving like a family friend and stop acting like someone who wants to see my marriage fall apart?" she questioned coaxingly.

"If that's what you wish, that's what you shall have. I just wanted Medwin to realize how lucky he was." Fletcher winked and placed a friendly kiss on her cheek. "Now back to the murder," he said in his best Boris Karloff imitation.

Marveling at Fletcher's ability to change roles with the ease with which someone else might change a pair of shoes, Melinda returned her attention to business.

They met up with John and the children in the dungeons. Immediately, Fletcher fell into step beside John and began a discussion of the Nicolus Blade books, complimenting John on his characterizations and plots.

Melinda felt a prickling sensation at the back of her neck as she and the children emerged onto the parade grounds. Glancing over her shoulder, she saw John watching her. Even through his impassive expression, she sensed his distrust. Breathing a silent sigh, she wished Fletcher wouldn't throw himself into every role so violently. It was very disconcerting for those who weren't used to him. Feeling as if she had her own little black cloud hanging over her, insistently preventing any sunlight from shining into her life, she guided the children into the gift shop and got change to buy sodas.

It was much later that night, after the children were in bed, when John sought her out. Coming into the den where she had been sitting in front of her typewriter staring at a blank sheet of paper for half an hour, he closed the door and regarded her grimly. "What kind of bribe did you offer

Fletcher to convince him to suddenly decide to be my very best friend?''

Catching the lurid suggestion in his voice, anger flashed in her eyes. ''I simply explained to him that I needed a friend who would be a friend to both me and you,'' she answered coolly. ''I told you he plays the roles he thinks his friends need him or want him to play.''

The grimness in John's features took on a strong cynical edge. ''Sort of like a chameleon.''

''He's unusual, but he cares about his friends,'' she snapped, her tone suggesting she doubted if John had any real feelings toward others. She expected him to make an equally cutting remark and stalk out of the room, but instead he shoved his hands into the pockets of his jeans and, leaning against the wall, studied her darkly. Certain the time had come for him to say he felt the marriage wasn't going to work and they'd have to make some arrangements to carry them through the next five years, she felt every muscle in her body tense. Attempting to steel herself against the inevitable, she told herself it was for the best to make the real break now. This way there would be no futile hoping for a future. But being reasonable didn't help. The knot in her stomach only tightened.

"Friends." John said the word gruffly, breaking the terse silence between them. "It has occurred to me that's where our problem lies. We never had time to become friends. We began our relationship in the middle." He paused for a moment as if he wanted to choose his next words carefully. "I think it would be best if we started again, this time at the beginning. But I don't think we can honestly do that and still share a bed. So, I'm going to move into the den for a while."

His attempt at diplomacy grated on Melinda's already taut nerves. "If you're bored with me, just say so. We don't have the soundest relationship in the world, but let's at least be honest with each other."

John's jaw hardened. "I'm being honest. I'll miss being in your bed. But like you said, we don't have the soundest relationship in the world. If this marriage is going to work, we have to try to build some sort of foundation.''

The reasoning tone in his voice only served to irritate her more. She knew he had a point, but his willingness to give her up as a lover hurt. I'm sure I've been a rather boring experience compared to his other women, she thought acidly. Aloud she said, "You're right. Enjoy the daybed." And with a dignity born of pride, she turned off her typewriter and left the room.

Chapter Ten

The next morning John looked as if he hadn't slept all night. Serves him right, Melinda thought, remembering the restless night she'd spent.

During those long hours, she'd told herself a million times she was better off without him. Early in life she'd taught herself to be self-reliant because she hadn't wanted to burden her brother. She was used to standing alone. "I don't need anyone else's strength or company," she stated aloud.

But in spite of her determined effort to convince herself she would be happier with him out of her life, she couldn't erase the emotions John had stirred within her. In the short time he'd shared her bed, she'd grown used to having him there. He was warm to lie against, and there was a curious comfort in waking to find him sleeping beside her.

Now she was alone again, only this time the aloneness was different. There was an aching that had never been there before.

Refusing to allow him to guess how deeply his desertion was hurting her, she maintained a wall of cool reserve during breakfast.

Following the meal, he insisted he, Frank and Joanie do the dishes. As she watched the three of them, the thought that John would never have had anything to do with her if it hadn't been for the children gnawed at her. A knot of pain formed in her abdomen. Furious with herself, she went into the den and tried to concentrate on her work.

A while later, she heard the front door open and close.

Then the den door opened and Frank stuck his head inside. "Uncle John had some errands to run," he informed her. "He said Joanie and I shouldn't bother you so we're going to watch *Mr. Rogers*."

"Thanks," Melinda muttered to empty space as Frank ducked back out immediately after delivering his message.

They even obey John better than they do me, she thought. Turning back to her work, she felt a wet trickle rolling down her cheek. Brushing it away with an angry swipe of her hand, she dared any more to follow. She'd done just fine before John Medwin had come into her life, and she'd do just fine when he left.

John returned while she was sitting in front of her twelfth try at beginning Chapter Five. When he entered the den, she momentarily considered completely ignoring him. But pride refused to allow her the coward's way out. Glancing over her shoulder with practiced nonchalance, she was about to deliver a cool, polite, very short greeting, when the words died on her lips.

Extending a bouquet of red roses mixed with baby's breath toward her, he said in a coaxing voice, "I was wondering if you would have dinner with me this evening. Harriet has agreed to look after the children, and I've made reservations at the Mansion. Harriet recommended it highly."

No, her little voice cried. It was better to make the break here and now. This marriage had been doomed from the start. The smart thing to do would be to work out some sort of arrangement whereby they would appear to be a happily married couple for the next five years while keeping their distance. But common sense failed to prevail. "Yes," she heard herself saying, knowing even as she said it she would live to regret this moment of weakness.

They dressed separately, keeping up the pretext of a couple going out on a date, as opposed to a husband and wife going out to dinner. Melinda suggested John dress first while she fed the children. This proved to be a major mistake. The lingering smell of his after-shave nearly drove her crazy while she applied her makeup.

Walking down the stairs, she felt like a teenager going out on her first date. You're only asking for trouble, her little voice warned as she forced a smile and said goodnight to Harriet and the children.

"You look very pretty tonight," John complimented her, breaking the silence that filled the car as they rode toward The Mansion.

"And you look very handsome," she returned. It was the truth. Even at the cocktail party in New Orleans he'd dressed in a pair of slacks, a turtleneck pullover and a sport coat. This was the first time she'd ever seen him in a suit and tie, and he did look exceptionally good. He also looked exceedingly uncomfortable, and she suddenly felt like the homely sister whose brother had talked an unwilling friend into taking her out. "It really isn't necessary for you to feel you have to put yourself through this agony," she said coolly, pride glistening in her eyes. She'd never forced herself on anyone and she wasn't going to start now. "We're two reasonable adults. I'm sure we can reach some sort of impersonal arrangement that will see us through the five years. There's no reason for you to have to suffer through my company this evening.''

John's jaw tensed. ''This isn't agony, and I don't consider being in your company something I must suffer through.''

''You look as uncomfortable as a man sitting on an anthill,'' she seethed, her nerves snapping. ''And I have no intention of spending the evening with someone who finds my company so unbearable.'' They had stopped at a light and her hand reached for the door handle. She'd call a taxi and go home before she'd ride another foot with John Medwin.

His hand caught hers before she could act. ''You're right, I'm uncomfortable. But not because of you. I hate wearing suits and ties. They don't feel natural on me. But I wanted tonight to be special....'' A self-consciousness crept into his voice as he continued gruffly. ''I meant it when I said I wanted us to be friends. It's easy for me to get close to the children. I trust them. They haven't yet learned to lie about their feelings. But getting close to another adult is difficult for me. I've spent my whole life working to keep a distance between myself and others.''

His honesty surprised her and threatened her guard. Studying his taut profile, she wondered if it was possible for him to tear down the barriers he'd built around himself. With every ounce of strength in her body she wanted him to try. "I'd like for us to be friends,'' she said levelly.

The muscles of his face relaxed visibly. ''I'm glad.'' He gave her hand a friendly squeeze before releasing it.

Warm currents shot up her arm. A sudden wave of resentment that he could so easily give up being her lover while her body still craved his so very much washed over her. Being his friend wasn't going to be easy.

The Mansion was an old estate home that had been converted into a restaurant. But in spite of its present commercial use, it had been furnished to maintain the graceful elegance of the house's history. They dined in a small room off what had once been the living room. Its windows fronted the house, and from the numerous bookshelves, Melinda guessed it had once served as the library. Because it was a small room, there were only four tables in it, thus providing a cozy, intimate atmosphere. During dinner they discussed music and types of movies and television shows they liked. Their tastes weren't always the same, but they weren't incompatible.

Melinda felt her guard slipping. Several times she almost found herself believing she was on a real date with a man who honestly wanted to be with her. During dessert, she made a quip that brought a genuine smile to his face. It was the gentlest, tenderest smile she'd ever seen and her heart pounded erratically for a moment. You're treading on dangerous ground, her inner voice warned, and this time she was smart enough not to totally ignore it.

During the ride home, she worked to rebuild her self-protective defenses. The dinner and companionship were a fantasy, she reminded herself curtly. Their separate rooms were a reality. For the children's sake, he was willing to try to be her friend. But that didn't mean he would ever want to share her bed again, and even if he did, it wouldn't be because he loved her. It would only be because he needed a warm body to share with his.

The children were already in bed asleep when they got home. For Harriet's sake Melinda put on a show of having a good time. Inwardly, she was already wishing she'd refused the date. She was only setting herself up to be hurt. As John left to walk Harriet home, she forced herself to face the full, futile truth. She wanted the impossible: She wanted John to learn to love her.

By the time he returned, she was exhausted from her inner struggles. Worried about what she might reveal in her tired and muddled state, she thanked him for the evening and, pleading a headache, escaped upstairs.

Entering her bedroom, she was again struck by how lonely it felt without him. Angrily pushing the thought out of her mind, she reached for the zipper at the back of her dress. But fits of temper and zippers don't mix well. The teeth snagged on a piece of fabric about four inches from her neck.

"Darn!" she swore under her breath, fighting back a threatening flood of tears. "Can't anything go right in my life?"

She tried to work it loose, but the zipper had caught in a spot that was hard to reach. The dress was one of her best, and she didn't want to put a hole in the delicate fabric by ripping the zipper loose. But the neck was high, and she couldn't slip the dress off unless she could get the zipper down farther. The only reasonable solution was to ask for help—but John was the only person available and she refused to turn to him. She was standing irresolutely in the middle of the floor, seriously contemplating ripping the dress off, when a knock sounded on the bedroom door. "Come in," she said, trying to keep the frustration out of her voice.

"I'm sorry to disturb you. I wanted my jeans and a pullover," John apologized as he entered. Crossing the room in long strides, he pulled out a fresh pair of jeans and a shirt from the closet.

His obvious discomfort at being in the bedroom they'd so recently shared grated on her already taut nerves. "You don't need to apologize for coming in here to get your clothes,'' she seethed.

He glanced toward her, obviously puzzled by her sudden foul humor.

"My zipper's stuck," she muttered, not wanting him to guess he had anything to do with her mood.

"Turn around," he ordered. Dropping his jeans and shirt on the bed, he began working with the zipper.

It took two full minutes for him to work the fabric loose, and they seemed like the two longest minutes of Melinda's life. She was acutely aware of his hands moving against her skin and his warm breath playing on the back of her neck. She was beginning to worry she might bite a hole through her lip in her efforts not to react to his touch, when the zipper finally came free.

"There," he said briskly. Picking up his clothes, he tossed a "Good night" over his shoulder and left the room as quickly as he had entered.

"Couldn't get away from me fast enough," she muttered hostilely, stripping off the dress and hanging it in the closet.

Sharply she recalled his reference to her as "poison."

Pulling out her nightgown, she still felt a warm tingling where his hands had brushed against her back and her self-directed anger built to volcanic proportions. How could she be so attracted to a man who was so immune to her?

Changing into her nightgown, she climbed into bed, but sleep refused to come. Every time she closed her eyes his image was there in her mind. For the next hour she tossed and turned and berated herself for caring so much. From the beginning she'd known they didn't have a chance. How could she have allowed herself to start loving the man?

She punched her pillow trying to rid herself of pent-up frustration. It didn't work.

Sleep was what she needed, she told herself. Tomorrow, when she was rested, she could be more rational, more practical, more in control. But the escape into sleep wouldn't come. Finally, every muscle aching, she gave up and climbed out of bed. She'd heard warm milk helped a person relax and, at this moment, she was willing to try anything.

Making her way quietly to the kitchen, she noticed the light in the den was off. Obviously John was having no trouble sleeping.

Turning on the small light near the sink, she found a pan. She was just about to pour the milk into it when the main light was suddenly switched on. Swinging around, she saw John standing in the doorway in his jeans. "I didn't mean to wake you," she apologized tightly.

Frowning, he gazed from the carton of milk to the pan. "Do you really drink that stuff heated?" he questioned with distaste.

"I was having a little trouble sleeping," she confessed grudgingly. "I heard it was supposed to help."

He combed his rumpled hair from his face with his fingers. "I was having a little trouble falling asleep myself. How about a few hands of gin rummy?"

"I don't think so." His bare chest was playing havoc with her senses and all she wanted was to escape before he guessed what effect he was having on her. Putting the pan back in the cabinet, she shoved the milk back in the refrigerator. "In fact, I don't think I even want the warm milk."

She moved toward the door, but he blocked her way. "I miss watching you sleep," he said gruffly. "You're cute the way you curl up and hug your pillow."

"It was your choice," she muttered, changing direction and leaving through the dining room.

He met her in the hall. "Maybe it was a bad choice."

She wanted him so badly her body ached, but the sting of his leaving her bed was too strong to ignore. "I wouldn't want you to do anything you'd regret in the morning," she said dryly.

A grimness came over his features. "Is that your way of saying you prefer things to remain this way?" he asked.

The anger that had been building inside her flashed in her eyes. If he expected her to invite him back into her bed, he'd have to wait for a cold day in hell. "You set the rules." Suddenly afraid she might say something to reveal how deeply he'd hurt her, she brushed past him and continued toward the stairs.

His hand closed around her upper arm like a vise. Jerking her up close to him, he looked down into her face. "If I made the rule, I can break it." Before she could protest, he tossed her over his shoulder and started up the stairs.

"Put me down," she hissed, keeping her voice low so she wouldn't wake the children.

Ignoring her demand, he carried her into the bedroom, gently kicking the door closed behind them. "I haven't had any sleep for two nights," he said, standing her on the floor in front of him. "Do you think we could continue to remain lovers while we work out this friendship business?"

Pride ordered her to say no. Taking him back into her bed would only be asking for new pain. Even more important, she wanted him to know what rejection felt like. But his hands on her waist were warm and her will where he was concerned was weak. "I don't know," she hedged. Fool! her little voice cried. You're only going to get hurt again if you give in. But she wasn't listening. He was kissing her neck and a bittersweet longing too intense to deny was urging her body to move into his embrace.

"You have the softest skin," he murmured, slipping her nightgown off and kissing her shoulder.

Even knowing in her heart she was only courting disaster, her hands sought the snap on his jeans. Tomorrow she knew she would regret this path but tonight she wanted him more than she'd ever wanted anything or anyone in her life.

For a long time after John fell asleep, Melinda lay watching him. He'd said he missed being in her bed. Probably what he meant was he missed having a warm body to satisfy his needs, her inner voice told her curtly.

"I don't care," she murmured and snuggling up against him, fell asleep.

But she did care. Melinda strongly regretted her weakness the next morning when she awoke to find herself alone. She couldn't believe how easily she'd melted into his arms at his slightest touch. Glancing at the clock, she saw it was nearly nine. "Frank and Joanie will be wanting breakfast," she muttered, trying to forget the growing feeling of humiliation her easy conquest was causing.

She climbed out of bed, dressed, and went downstairs. The coffee was made and the children informed her John had already fed them.

Chewing on the inside of her bottom lip, she started toward the den. She knew he was in there; she could hear his typewriter clicking.

But before she reached the door, she stopped. She wasn't ready to face him this morning.

Pouring herself a cup of coffee, she carried it into the living room. Sinking into an old overstuffed chair, she stared with unseeing eyes at the opposite wall. I wasn't wanton. I'm his wife. I'm supposed to share my bed with him, she told herself. But it didn't help. Her hands balled into fists. I should've put up some kind of a struggle!

"I thought I heard you wandering around." John's voice broke the stillness of the room.

Melinda's body tensed as he moved toward her chair. She willed herself to speak, to say something . . . anything. But no sound came out.

"You were sleeping so peacefully this morning I didn't want to wake you," he was saying in a warm tone. With his hands on either arm of the chair, he leaned forward and kissed her lightly. "Now that you're up, what would you like to do today? When you answer, keep in mind that it'll be just you and me. I hope you don't mind, but I've arranged with Harriet to have her watch the children. I thought we needed more time alone to work on becoming friends."

The warmth in his eyes caused a small seed of hope to germinate within her. Finding her voice, she said, "I'd like that."

When she couldn't come up with an itinerary for the day, he did. First he took her out to breakfast. After that, they went car shopping. "We need a second car," he informed her. "Something big enough for trips. Frank tells me you like the beach."

"I do," she admitted.

"Then we should get something with four-wheel drive. I've heard there are some great spots a person can get to down at Hatteras if they have the right kind of transportation." His voice was filled with purpose and Melinda suddenly felt as if she'd been caught up in a tornado.

They purchased a Bronco that afternoon, to be picked up the next day. On the way home, John informed her he'd made reservations for them at Nags Head, and two days later she found herself, the children and Harriet being driven by John toward the eastern shore. He'd insisted on Harriet coming with them. "I was able to book a two-room suite," he explained. "I want time alone with you, but Frank and Joanie would never forgive us if we went to the shore without them. So, Harriet is going to come along to watch over them."

Sitting beside him, Melinda studied his boxer's profile. He's trying too hard, her little voice whispered. If he really cared, he wouldn't have to try so hard. She forced the thought out of her mind but it kept popping back in.

During the next few days they played on the beach, climbed the dunes, hunted shells, toured Kitty Hawk and flew kites on the beach. They laughed a lot, and on the surface everyone seemed to be having a wonderful time.

But below the surface, Melinda wasn't so certain things were going well. It was impossible for her not to notice that when John was with the children he was completely relaxed but when he was alone with her there was a fine line of restraint.

On their last day, the children insisted on building a gigantic sand castle. Everyone ended up helping, and when it was done, it was nearly five feet tall.

"Penny for your thoughts," John offered, as he and Melinda sat on the warm sand watching Joanie and Frank adding decorative touches to their finished castle under Harriet's supervision.

"I was wondering if they'll be disappointed tomorrow when they discover the tide has washed away all of their hard work," she replied.

"I don't think so. They're used to finding their castles gone," he answered thoughtfully.

"I suppose," she conceded. The sun was warm and the sky was clear blue. The sea gulls played on the breeze while waves lapped at the shore. All in all, it was a perfect day, she thought lazily. It was even more perfect because John was beside her. She felt so complete with him near her. She shook herself back to reality. Don't start building castles in the clouds, she admonished herself. They're even less substantial than sand ones. In spite of the heat on this hot summer day, a chill shook her. It was very difficult not to daydream in this vacation environment. "Some castles are harder to lose than others." The warning to herself slipped out unexpectedly.

"They'll survive," he assured her. "And you need to learn to relax." Gently he began massaging her shoulders.

He had the most soothing hands. If she were a cat, she would've purred. She knew it was dangerous, but for just this day she wanted to live in her fantasy. She wanted to believe he could learn to love her. Just for today, she promised herself. Closing her eyes, she let his touch fill her senses.

Chapter Eleven

Reality, Melinda decided the morning of her second day back home, is for the birds.

Her agent had called that morning to say that while her book was selling well, it mostly likely wasn't going to make the best-sellers' list. "But why should you care about a small thing like that when you have John?" Ruth had said in an attempt to ease the blow.

If she'd really had John, she wouldn't, Melinda agreed mentally. But while he continued to be attentive, she couldn't stop feeling he was making the effort for the children, not for himself. Hiding her disappointment, aloud she said philosophically, "Maybe next time."

That phone call was followed almost immediately by one from Fletcher. "First the good news," he said cheerfully. "The tickets went so fast, we're already planning a second night of murder and mayhem. The caterers are contracted and the cleaning crew has gone through the place with their busy little brooms."

"What's the bad news?" she coaxed when he made what he called a pregnant pause.

Fletcher's voice became serious. "Adelle bought a ticket. To be more correct, she bought two tickets, but I don't know who she's bringing."

A foreboding chill ran down Melinda's spine. "I wonder what she's up to."

"I've considered the possibilities and have concluded that you shouldn't worry too greatly. We've got the cream of Wilmington society coming. Even the governor and a couple of our congresspersons have purchased tickets. She'll have to be on her best behavior. It's only to a few of us that she shows her true colors. She has a reputation she wants to maintain with the others.''

"I hope he's right," Melinda muttered as she hung up the phone.

"You hope who's right about what?" John asked.

Spinning around, she found him leaning against the wall a couple of feet away.

"I didn't mean to eavesdrop, but you sounded worried," he apologized.

"I am a little." Leaning against the opposite wall, she said grimly, "Adelle has bought tickets to the murder. She's probably just coming because she knows her presence will spoil the evening for me. But I don't trust her, so I can't be certain she won't try something to embarrass me. She's got a real mean streak in her."

"Would it ease your mind to know I'll be there to protect you?" he questioned.

Her eyes widened in surprise. "You will?"

"Bought my ticket the day after I found out about the event. Couldn't have my wife wandering around that old place at night without her protector."

There was a softness in his eyes that made her heart skip a beat. "I'm glad you're going to be there."

A self-conscious smile played at the corners of his mouth. "Part of our agreement was that I'm to protect you from the evil witch."

"Yes, I suppose it is." The momentary joy she'd experienced vanished with his reference to the basis behind their marriage. Still, she was glad he would be there.

By opening night, she was as nervous as a cat. Worries about Adelle were relegated to the back of her mind while she agonized over the script. Fletcher had assured her it played well, but still she worried that the audience would be disappointed.

"Audiences haven't stoned authors in centuries," John teased as they rode an early ferry across to the fort.

"They didn't have Adelle to lead them," she tossed back, a vision of the woman casting the first stone coming sharply into her mind.

John's manner became serious as he placed his arm around her shoulders. "I'll protect you," he promised solemnly.

Glancing up into his face, she saw the sincerity of his remark etched into his features so strongly it brought a pleased flush to her face. "I'll remember that," she said huskily. It was as if a warm, safe blanket had been wrapped around her shoulders. Going up on tiptoe, she placed a light thank-you kiss on his lips.

A warmth burned in his eyes. "I'll extract a fee for services rendered later tonight," he assured her, kissing the hollow behind her ear.

Her body ignited, then the ferry lurched as it turned and began maneuvering into docking position, and once again her blood turned cold with fear. It was almost time for the curtain to rise.

They arrived at the fort to find Fletcher and Valerie Suterfield already there. Valerie, a pleasant woman in her mid-fifties devoted to preserving historical sites in Delaware, was acting as hostess. She'd been in charge of organizing the entire affair, and her position as a matriarch of Wilmington society was part of the reason for its success.

Since Valerie was a widow, Fletcher was acting as official host. "It'll be wonderful," he reassured Melinda. "Relax and enjoy the evening. You've earned it."

"Yes, dear," Valerie seconded enthusiastically. She turned toward John and her hand went to the mass of white hair gathered in ringlets on top of her head to make certain they were still in place. "And I am so pleased to meet you, Mr. Medwin. My late husband read all of your books."

John smiled and Melinda saw Valerie's flush deepen with pleasure. She's fascinated by him, Melinda mused grudgingly. She'd thought he looked especially good in his dinner jacket, but then, he looked good to her all of the time. I just wish other women didn't find him so appealing, she admitted wryly.

Adelle arrived with a man. Although he was dressed in formal attire as opposed to Bermuda shorts and a loud shirt, Melinda was certain he was the man who had posed

as the tourist in the hallway outside her hotel room door in New Orleans. That morning had been one of the more traumatic of
her life and every detail was strongly etched
into her mind. The guests had been asked
not to bring cameras, but Melinda couldn't
help noticing that the man toyed with his
cigarette lighter a great deal, and she remembered seeing detective shows where the
characters had used cameras concealed in
similar lighters. "You've been watching too
much television," she chided herself under
her breath. Besides, as long as she acted
natural and didn't allow Adelle to provoke
her, there would be nothing for the man to
photograph even if he did have a concealed
camera.

Melinda had almost convinced herself she
had everything under control when Denise
McQuay arrived. Until this evening, she
knew of Denise only by reputation. The
woman was wealthy in her own right, exceptionally beautiful and enjoyed a freewheel-
ing existence. Fletcher called her The Vamp,
pronouncing the words as if they were capi-
talized. "She'll go after any man she finds

attractive,'' he'd told Melinda once. Because he was a recognized talent in the local theater and just eccentric enough to be interesting but not embarrassing, he was an included guest at many parties given by the upper crust. Thus, he'd had many opportunities to observe Denise in action. ''She seems to prefer married men, and she usually gets what she goes after,'' he'd finished.

Melinda didn't doubt this latest statement one tiny bit. Immediately upon her arrival at the fort, Denise headed straight for John. And she'd done her homework. She was the only guest who didn't launch into a discussion of John's books. Instead, she brought up his interest in conservation.

''I do hope you're going to involve yourself with our water pollution problems. We have quite a few oil tankers coming up the Delaware River, and lately we've begun to have more and more problems with oil spills,'' she said, holding on to John's hand a little longer than a polite handshake required. She was wearing a fiery red off-the-shoulder dress that fitted like a second skin. A slit up the right side to the top of her thigh allowed her to move while at the same time exposing a long, attractive line of leg. Coal black hair fell to her shoulders, framing an exotically beautiful face with a full-lipped, sensual mouth. Beside her, Melinda felt pale and insignificant.

Glad of the change of subject, John fell into an easy conversation on the dangers of oil pollution. Artfully, Denise managed to exclude Melinda from the discussion. She even managed to ease herself between Melinda and John, making Melinda look like the outsider.

Seeing other people glancing toward them, Melinda's pride insisted she play the part of the trusting wife. "If you'll excuse me," she said, her face feeling brittle as she offered a superficial smile, "I think I see some old friends."

Moving away, she said hello to a couple in the far corner, then made her way toward the punch. Glancing over her shoulder, she noticed Denise had slipped her arm through John's as if staking a permanent claim. I wonder how she'd like a swim in the moat, Melinda mused acidly, plotting out a plan to lure the woman outside. But with the grip she has on John, she'd probably take him with her, she noted and scrapped the idea.

"Do you really think it's safe to leave John with The Vamp?" Fletcher said, coming up beside her. "When she's really hot, she's a bit hard for any man to resist."

"Maybe you're right," she conceded, her stomach knotting as Denise laughed and swayed toward John. "Even a trusting wife can only take so much."

An impatient scowl darkened Fletcher's features as he continued to watch Denise's antics. "If we don't break them up, no one is going to notice our players beginning trysts. Our audience might even miss our murders."

With Fletcher at her side, Melinda approached John and Denise. "I've come to reclaim my husband," she said, smiling and slipping her arm through John's unclaimed arm.

"And I've come at the request of several of our male guests," Fletcher said in the most charming manner as he claimed Denise's free arm and wrapped it around his.

"They offered to donate another ten dollars each if I walk you across the room. They've got bets on how high your dress is slit." He smiled down at her coaxingly. "I know you'll do anything for a good cause."

"Sometimes, even for a bad one," Denise returned with a playful laugh. Turning her attention to John, she said, "I hope to continue this discussion at a later time," and releasing her hold on his arm, walked slowly across the room with Fletcher.

Melinda bit back a catty remark that almost slipped off the tip of her tongue. Pride refused to allow her jealousy to show. Glancing up at John, she saw the anger in his eyes belying the polite smile on his face and her stomach knotted tighter. He was angry because Fletcher had taken Denise away.

Suddenly the play began with a shouting match between two of the players. After that, each guest was given a flashlight to carry and the tour of the fort began.

Melinda tried not to think about Denise and John but the effort was futile. The woman was persistent and as the guests climbed the spiral staircase Melinda discovered Denise had managed to work herself up beside John.

"It's always nice to have a man's strong arm nearby when one is on this uneven terrain," she said, falling into step on John's right as they reached the battlements. "I hope your wife won't mind."

Melinda wanted to threaten the woman with her life if she didn't keep her hands off John. But instead she said with forced politeness, "Won't your date be lonely?"

"Alas, I came alone." Denise's mouth formed a pretty pout. "Arthur has the flu but I refused to miss this opportunity to meet the famous John Medwin." She put a strong emphasis on the word *famous* while smiling up at John with adoring eyes.

John met the flattery with a casual laugh while Melinda again found herself wondering how much he missed the variety of companionship he'd been used to.

As they descended the stairs and began to make their way through the second level, Denise flashed her light into the dark corners. "These old passages scare me. You never know what will fly out at you," she said with just the right mingling of fear and excitement in her voice.

Melinda was tempted to say she was under the impression Denise wasn't afraid of anything that went bump in the night. Instead she said, "I'm sure nothing will fly out at us."

Suddenly letting out a scream, Denise flung herself into John's arms.

"What did you see?" he questioned in calming tones, as the other guests frantically flashed their lights around looking for whatever had frightened the woman.

"Silly me. It must have been just a shadow." With a giggle to suggest embarrassment toward her uncalled-for fright, Denise slowly released her hold on John. Trailing her hands over his shoulders in a suggestive caress, she said, "But it was nice to have such strong arms to protect me."

Even if she hadn't noticed Adelle's companion frantically playing with his cigarette lighter, Melinda's nerves would have snapped. "Really, Denise. Your exaggerated dramatics are adolescent," she said sharply. "If you keep them up, people are going to think you're part of the murder and I don't want anyone thinking I would write such garbage.''

Denise's disruption had brought the entire tour to a halt. Leaving his position as leader, Fletcher made his way to the trio just as Melinda delivered her cut. "And I hate being upstaged," he said with strong reprimand. Then the anger was replaced by a charming smile as he added, "Therefore, I insist that you, my delightfully gorgeous wench, come with me to the front of the line. If you again feel the need to fall into strong arms, I want them to be mine.''

Everyone laughed and the tension Denise's scream had caused eased.

With another smile cast in John's direction, Denise slipped her arm through Fletcher's and allowed herself to be led away.

"Don't look so concerned," John said dryly as the tour began to move once again. "I'm certain Denise's theatrics haven't harmed your script.''

"I'm only sorry I didn't include an unexplained murder of one of the guests," Melinda seethed under her breath.

To her relief, the trek through the dungeons was uneventful. A bar and a long table filled with hors d'oeuvres greeted them when they emerged onto the parade ground.

Stepping up to a microphone set up near the bar, Fletcher called the guests to gather around him. "Important clues are to be found in the prisoners' quarters," Fletcher informed the guests. "You'll be taken in small groups by the Rangers—" he paused to wave an arm toward the two uniformed men to his left "—and given approximately fifteen minutes to observe the premises. Please don't remove anything...simply *observe*. While you're waiting for your turn, and after you've had a chance to inspect the quarters, we hope you'll entertain yourself by enjoying these tasty offerings." He waved an arm toward the bar and table in an inviting manner. Then, pulling a sheet of paper from his pocket, he called out a list of names of guests who were to be in the first group.

Melinda's and John's names were on that list. To Melinda's relief, Denise's was not. But her relief was short-lived. As they reached the quarters, Melinda heard Adelle's voice.

"I just couldn't wait. I've really gotten caught up in the game," Adelle was saying in a laughing voice to one of the older couples. Her eyes danced toward Melinda as she added, "And I'm determined to win."

Still tense from Denise's attempts to seduce John, Melinda wasn't certain if her control would hold through another battle. It has to, she told herself curtly, watching as Adelle made her way toward her and John.

They were in the room that had once served as a prison for Confederate officers. Coming to a halt in front of Melinda and John, Adelle let her eyes roam over the walls, then come to rest on John. "You must feel right at home here since you, too, are a prisoner...." She paused to allow her analogy to sink in. So her comment would sound innocent to those who might have overheard, she finished, "Of love, that is. But I've heard one type of prison is very like another in the final analysis."

From the hush that fell in their immediate vicinity, it was obvious several people were listening. Melinda felt a flush building from her neck upward. She wanted to say something to counter Adelle's cut, but it had sliced too close to the truth and words refused to come.

It was John who responded. Smiling charmingly, he slipped an arm around Melinda's shoulders as he met Adelle's malicious gaze with quiet calm. "That depends on the person doing the analysis. I'm quite happy with my entrapment."

"Of course you are." Adelle returned his smile but the look in her eyes called him a liar. Then, waving to some friends across the room, she left them.

Watching her walk away, Melinda felt a huge lump in her throat. How she wished he really meant those words.

She spent the next couple of hours waiting for a second attack by Adelle, but it never came: It wasn't necessary, she thought acidly, as Fletcher revealed the murderer and the motive. The one encounter had successfully ruined her evening.

Even when Fletcher finally announced the evening was over and the guests applauded the cast and proclaimed they'd had a wonderful time, Melinda's spirits weren't heightened. Every time she looked at John, she pictured him trapped in a prison with walls even more sturdy than those of this fort.

"A raving success," Fletcher said cheerfully, joining her at her table.

"Yes," she answered absently, watching John as he walked to the coffee table to get them both another cup while they waited for their turn on the ferry. She and John were scheduled for the fourth crossing. The guests scheduled for the third crossing were gathering near the door. Denise was one of them. While Melinda watched, the woman left her group for a moment and approached John. Melinda could not make out what Denise said, but she did see the dark-haired beauty slip a piece of paper into John's pocket.

Fletcher's expression darkened as he followed Melinda's line of vision. "If I didn't know Denise would go for John on her own initiative, I'd swear Adelle put her up to it."

"It doesn't matter why she's trying so hard to seduce him," Melinda replied tightly. "What matters is if—" She'd been going to say, "if he's tempted," but the thought was too painful to say aloud.

Fletcher squeezed her hand reassuringly. "He's a fool if he'd risk losing you."

"Congratulations," John addressed both of them upon his return to the table. "Your evening seems to have been a smashing success."

Accepting her coffee, Melinda studied him covertly. On the surface he was politeness personified. But she couldn't shake the uneasiness she sensed behind the facade. "I'm just glad it's over," she said honestly. "From now on, Fletcher is on his own. The author only has to show up for opening night."

A chorus of goodbyes came from the doorway as the guests gathered there were told the jitney was waiting.

Waving to the group, Fletcher watched the hips in the tight red dress move sensually as their owner followed her fellow passengers. "I told Denise to let me know in advance if she was planning to attend any more of my functions. I promised to have a part written in for her."

As a victim, Melinda promised herself mentally, enjoying the thought of killing off the woman.

The wait for the ferry and the ride across the river were made easier by the cast. They joined John, Melinda and Fletcher and re-hashed what they thought went over best and what needed to be improved.

But during the drive home from Delaware City, when John and Melinda were once again alone, the silence in the car became ominously heavy. Melinda tried to think of something to say, but she couldn't get her mind off the piece of paper in John's pocket or Adelle's reference to him as a prisoner.

"Do you want to take the first shower or shall I?" he questioned curtly when they arrived home.

"You go ahead," she answered, heading for the kitchen to take a couple of aspirin. It'd been a long evening. Too long.

When she went upstairs a few minutes later, she discovered him still working on getting himself out of his evening clothes. The jacket and pants had been tossed onto a chair and he was removing studs from the shirt.

Looking at the discarded pants, Melinda's control snapped. Picking them up, she slipped her hand into the pocket and pulled out the slip of paper. It had a phone number on it. "Are you going to call her?" she questioned stiffly.

His gaze narrowed challengingly. "I'm surprised you even asked. The way you walked off and left me to her, I got the distinct impression you really don't care what I do."

Her jaw trembled. "Of course I care." Afraid of revealing more about her feelings than she wanted to, she added quickly, "Denise likes to brag about her conquests. If you have an affair with her, Adelle will have her on the witness stand testifying that our marriage is a sham before the sheets have time to cool."

Cynicism etched itself into his features. "In other words, you don't care what I do or who I do it with as long as it isn't made public." Discarding the shirt, he strode into the bathroom before she could offer a response.

Staring at the closed door, she pictured him alone with the seductive Denise. Melinda couldn't blame him. She'd practically invited him to do it. "No!" The word came out with firm resolve. She kicked off her shoes, walked into the bathroom and stepped into the shower.

"What the devil?" he growled, watching the water soak her hair and dress.

She faced him levelly. "I believe very strongly in the sanctity of marriage. If you had an affair or even a one-night stand, I would feel betrayed."

The anger in his eyes softened. "I'm glad to hear that. I wouldn't like to think my resistance to other women's wiles was an unappreciated strain."

His admission that he found other women attractive hurt. "I'm sorry it's such a strain for you," she said tersely.

"It's not such a strain," he assured her. His eyes followed the lines of her body, now plastered with the fabric of her dress. "I think your dress is ruined."

"It's drip-dry," she muttered, starting to leave the shower.

He caught her by the shoulders. "Stay." The word came out husky, and looking up, she saw the soft brown coaxing in his eyes.

"I've never peeled a woman out of a dress before," he said, his hands seeking the zipper.

She had no will to resist him. "Well, I wouldn't want to deprive either of us of a new experience," she muttered, kissing his wet shoulder.

Chapter Twelve

Three weeks after the murder, Melinda sat in the den listening to the silence surrounding her. School had started and Joanie and Frank were in their respective classrooms for seven hours a day on weekdays. But even when they were home, the house held a void. John was gone.

A little over a week earlier he'd told her he had a deadline to meet for his latest book and was having writer's block. He'd said he hated leaving her and the children, but he felt he could work better at his place in

Pennsylvania. She knew how difficult writer's block could be and had forced herself to cheerfully agree. But she missed him horribly.

So did the children. Frank asked about him constantly, and every day when he returned home from school, he looked around the house to see if John had returned. When the phone rang, Frank was the first person to answer it, always hoping it was his uncle.

John's calls were irregular. If his work was going well, he might miss a day. Once he had called late at night. "I know it's late," he'd apologized. "But I lost track of the time and I wanted to make certain everything was all right with you and the children."

"We're just fine," she'd assured him. She always had to bite her tongue to keep from saying how much they missed him and asking when he would be returning. But she promised herself she would put no pressure on him. He'd given up a great deal for her and the children. She wouldn't interfere with his writing.

But this morning's call had been different. He had asked her to come up for the weekend. She should have been ecstatic. But there had been an underlying tension in his voice that nagged at her. Something was wrong. "You're overreacting," she told herself. "He's probably just tense from his writing."

But the self-assurance didn't help. There was no use trying to ignore it or deny it...she was worried about losing him. It wasn't a new worry, but it had been growing steadily stronger with his absence, and the underlying tension in his voice this morning had nourished it. Pushing her chair away from her desk, she rose and paced across the room. He had become such a big part of her life. She doubted she would ever be able to fill the void his leaving would create.

"You're making a mountain out of a molehill," she chided herself aloud, hoping that hearing the words spoken would give them more validity. It didn't.

Raking a hand through her hair, she stared out the window with unseeing eyes.

The ringing of the doorbell made her jump. Any interruption would be a welcome relief to this worrying, she thought as she went to answer it. But she was wrong. She sighed mentally as she opened the door to find Adelle on the other side.

"Aren't you going to invite me in?" the woman asked sweetly.

Melinda sensed trouble. Of course, she always sensed trouble when Adelle made an appearance. "The children are in school," she said coolly.

"It's you I've come to see." Adelle's smile sweetened even further. "I've come to bury the hatchet."

Where? was the question that popped into Melinda's head. She was in no mood to deal with Adelle today, but the determination in Adelle's eyes told her there was no way out. Stepping aside, she allowed the woman to enter.

Adelle sauntered into the living room and seated herself in one of the wing-back chairs. She was wearing a demure blue suit with all of the accessories, including a hat and gloves.

The phrase "dressed to kill" came to Melinda's mind. Well, I won't die easily! Crossing the room, she seated herself in the chair facing Adelle. "And to what do I owe this visit?"

"I've come to thank you."

Adelle's smile did not reach her eyes, and it was those cold, calculating eyes that Melinda watched as she said, "Thank me for what?"

"I never thought your marriage to John Medwin would prove to be so beneficial to me."

Adelle laughed lightly and Melinda thought of the witches stirring the caldron in *Macbeth*. "Beneficial?"

"I knew I only had to wait. You are rather boring for a man like John Medwin, my dear. But I never expected him to be so generous."

Melinda's stomach twisted into a hard, tight knot. "Generous?"

"I'd call fifty thousand dollars generous, wouldn't you?" Adelle's eyes glistened with pleasure.

Bile rose in Melinda's throat. "He gave you fifty thousand dollars?"

"I picked up the check this morning from his lawyer," Adelle confirmed. "It's not flattering to admit, but we all have our price. I know you'll be relieved to learn I've given up all claims to the children. They're yours."

Mock sympathy came over Adelle's features. "John told me you didn't know about our little business transaction. He also made it clear I wasn't to tell you. He wants to tell you himself. But while we've had our differences, I only felt it was fair to give you warning."

Rising from her chair, Adelle stood looking down at Melinda. "He's paid handsomely for his freedom. I hope you'll face this like a lady and give him his divorce without any theatrics." Moving toward the door, she added, "Don't worry about showing me out. I can find my way. Have a nice day, Melinda."

For a long time after Adelle left, Melinda sat staring at the empty chair across from her. She wanted to believe Adelle was lying, but she knew she wasn't. John had bought himself out of the marriage.

He was going to tell her this weekend what he had done, and ask for a divorce. That explained the underlying tension in his invitation. You knew it was going to happen when he never brought up the subject of having children of our own again, she told herself curtly.

Her mind went back to the night of the murder play at the fort. Adelle must have struck a strong chord when she referred to him as a prisoner. And then there had been Denise. John had even admitted he had to fight the attraction he felt toward other women. Obviously he'd decided the struggle wasn't worth the effort it required. Her hands balled into fists as she wondered if he'd spent the last week alone. Probably not, her little voice answered, forcing her to face the full brunt of the pain she had opened herself up to by falling in love with the man.

If I could cry, it would help, she thought frantically. But her hurt was too intense for tears. She felt nauseated and her body trembled.

She glanced toward the clock. She had been sitting in shock for nearly half an hour. She had to pull herself together!

Closing her eyes, she forced herself to think. She should be grateful to Adelle for giving her this opportunity to prepare herself. It would have been humiliating to break down in front of John like this.

Slowly, anger replaced her pain. He should have come to her. He should have told her he was unhappy. She would have tried to work something out that wouldn't have cost him so dearly. Her jaw hardened into a firm line. She would do what she had always planned to do when the children started going to school full days. She would find a good job, a steady job with benefits and a pension. In her spare time and evenings she would write. And she would pay John back every cent—for both the money he'd given Adelle and the money he'd spent on household expenses during their short-lived marriage.

Determination and pride glistened in her eyes. But the first thing she was going to do was move John out of her home. He obviously didn't want to come back, so she would make certain he didn't have to.

Picking up the phone, she punched in Harriet's number. For a moment after the ring was answered on the other end, her vocal cords froze. Forcing them to work, she mumbled a hello, then said with artificial calm, "Could you look after the children for a few days for me?"

"You don't sound like yourself," Harriet's worried voice came over the line. "Is something wrong?"

"No," Melinda lied. She couldn't bring herself to tell anyone, not even Harriet, what had happened. Knowing that Harriet would require some sort of explanation, she said, "I want to go up and see John."

"Now that sounds like a good idea. I've never felt it was good for couples to be separated too long at any one time if it could be avoided," Harriet said cheerfully. "Don't you worry about the children. I love looking after them."

"Thanks," Melinda managed, then hung up before Harriet could ask any more questions.

Going upstairs, she found John's suitcases. She was busy shoving his clothing into them when Harriet suddenly appeared at the bedroom door.

"I called out but you must have been too preoccupied to hear me. I thought I would come over and offer my help with your packing, and I need to know when the children catch their bus and..." The older woman's voice trailed off as her eyes came to rest on John's clothes haphazardly crammed into the luggage. Frowning with concern, she shifted her gaze to Melinda. "What's going on?"

Continuing to shove John's clothing into the bags, Melinda told her about Adelle's visit. "And so I'm saving him the trouble of packing. I'm moving him out. I'm going to load all of his belongings into my car and drive them up to him," she finished through clenched teeth. "And that will be the end of John Medwin in our lives!"

"What about the children?" Harriet questioned worriedly. "They've grown very fond of him."

"They'll survive," she answered tersely. "I'll tell them his writing is his work and he couldn't do it here. Luckily he wasn't in our lives too long. They'll forget about him soon enough."

The concern on Harriet's face deepened. "What about you? Are you going to be all right?"

"I'm going to be just fine," Melinda assured her with cold control. "As far as I'm concerned, he's already out of my life."

Walking around the bed, Harriet gave Melinda a hug. "This has been a shock. I don't think you should drive up there alone."

Melinda's jaw hardened with resolve. "I have to go. It began there and it will end there."

"I suppose we should look at the bright side," Harriet said encouragingly. "You don't have to worry about Adelle any longer."

Melinda nodded stiffly. "I have Frank and Joanie and that's all I wanted in the first place." Snapping the suitcases shut, she picked them up and carried them downstairs.

By the time the children arrived home from school, Melinda had everything of John's packed into her car.

"Harriet is going to take care of you for the next few days," she explained as she fed them milk and cookies. She forced her voice to sound casual. She didn't want to upset them. "I'm going up to see Uncle John."

"Bring him back. I miss him," Frank said, looking up at her pleadingly.

"He can even grow his beard back," Joanie offered.

Melinda saw the anxiety in the children's eyes. Obviously they, too, had sensed there was more to John's absence than his merely getting away to write. They'll survive, she told herself again. And so will I! Giving them each a tight hug and a kiss, she said, "It's a long drive and I need to get started. You two be real good for Harriet."

"I still don't like the idea of you driving all that way alone," Harriet protested worriedly, following her out to her car.

"I need the time alone," Melinda confessed, and giving the woman a goodbye hug, she climbed in and drove away.

It was well after dark when she stopped and found a motel room. But nerves taut with anger and a sense of betrayal kept her from getting any rest, and she resumed her drive in the small hours of the morning. He had done the honorable thing, her rational mind pointed out. He'd made certain she would have the children. But she couldn't be rational about this. Not now, anyway. The fact that he'd been so desperate to end their marriage that he'd been willing to pay Adelle fifty thousand dollars hurt so deeply she doubted the wound would ever heal. All she could hope to do was get through this meeting with dignity. It was going to take some time to get her emotions back in the proper perspective. Mentally she rehearsed a hundred versions of what she would say to him and how she would say it. She would be cool—polite with just the right touch of indifference.

As she neared the entrance to his property, the fear of finding him with someone else almost caused her to turn back and phone him first. But telling herself the shock of actually seeing him with another woman would help stop the hurt faster, she went on.

Her legs felt weak as she swung the gate open. She didn't want to face him. But pride forced her on.

Dawn was breaking over the horizon when she parked in front of the house. The Bronco and his Jeep were the only other cars there. But that didn't mean he didn't have company. He'd given Melinda a key to his house, but using it was out of the question. If he was here with another woman, she didn't want to actually see them in bed together.

She considered marching up to the door and knocking. Then, in her mind's eye, she visualized a woman in something skimpy answering and a cold chill shook her. Admitting that her earlier show of bravery had been a charade, she took the coward's way out. She decided to unload John's belongings onto the porch before she made her presence known. That way, when she did finally face him, she would only have to take the time to tell him she would pay him back every cent he had spent on her and the children, including all the money he'd given Adelle, then she could leave.

She was setting her second load down on the porch beside the first when she heard the door opening. Her heart caught in her throat as she turned around and saw John.

Unshaven, wearing a pair of hastily pulled-on jeans, he stared at her with sleep-blurred eyes. "I didn't expect you for a couple of days," he said groggily. Then, rubbing the sleep from his eyes, he asked, "And what's all this stuff?"

Her chin threatened to tremble at the sight of him. She had known seeing him would be difficult, but she'd never imagined it could be this painful. The hurt fed her anger and the urge to scream at him was strong. But she was determined to behave with dignity. "They're your belongings," she answered coolly.

His gaze narrowed. "What did you intend to do, just dump them on the porch and leave?"

Pride glistened in her eyes. "No. But I didn't know if you had a friend visiting, and if so, I didn't want to disturb the two of you too early in the morning." The moment the words were out, she wished she'd never said them. She should have stopped with a simple no. She didn't really want to know if he had another woman with him. She was in enough pain. "If you'll get out of my way, I'll finish unloading my car."

But he didn't move. "I don't have a friend visiting," he said levelly. He was watching her, but his expression gave away nothing. "Can I assume Adelle paid a call on you yesterday?"

"Yes." Bile rose in her throat. She swallowed it back. "And I'm glad she did. She saved you a trip back to Wilmington. I'm sorry you felt you had to pay out so much money for your freedom, but I'll pay you back. It will take a while, but you'll get every cent." A lump was forming in her throat. She had to get away from him before she lost control and made a fool of herself! "I need to start home soon. I'll finish unloading your things and then be on my way."

"Wait just one minute!" he ordered, his hand closing around her wrist as she started past him.

The heat of his touch broke her control. Jerking free, she took a step back. "Please, don't touch me." The request came out as a snarl. Damn! She cursed her weakness toward the man as hot tears flooded her eyes. He was bound to realize how much she was hurting. It didn't matter now if she ran. Practically flying past him, she raced toward her car. She should have sent his things back with a letter. Anything would have been better than facing him and making a fool of herself!

"Melinda." Catching up with her, he captured her by the shoulders. Looking hard into her face, he said tersely, "I want a chance to explain."

She tried to jerk free but his grip was like steel. "Please." The word came out weakly as she stared at the ground, refusing to look up into his face. She couldn't stand to see the pity in his eyes. She didn't want to hear his apology about how he'd tried but was bored by their marriage, bored by her. "Just let me go. It's over. I appreciate what you did for me and Joanie and Frank but I don't want any postmortems. In our hearts we both knew the marriage had very little chance of succeeding." Her voice almost caught on the word *hearts*. She had to get away! Frantically, she tried to pull free.

His fingers bit into her as his grip tightened even further. "I didn't pay Adelle off to buy my freedom."

She stopped struggling. Anger mingled with disbelief deep within her. "Don't lie to me. There is no other reason." To her despair hot tears escaped and rolled down her cheeks. Humiliated, she had to be free. With the instinct of an animal fighting for its survival, she kicked him hard in the shin. Pain registered on his face and his hold slackened. Twisting free, she again raced for the car. She'd mail the rest of his things to him. Right now all she wanted was to get away.

But John's hand closed around her arm as she reached for the door handle. Jerking her around, he pinned her against the vehicle. "In spite of the fact that you've probably cracked my shinbone, I love you, Melinda," he said gruffly.

Her jaw trembled. Her very soul had ached to hear him say those words. Now he'd said them but she couldn't believe him. "You paid Adelle fifty thousand dollars to give up her claim to the children," she pointed out tersely. "If our marriage was going to work, there was no need."

Releasing her arm, he took a step backward. Regarding her grimly, he said, "You're wrong. I had a very strong need. I cared too much." Self-consciousness entered his voice. "I've always cared. After I returned here from New Orleans I couldn't get you off my mind. I'd find myself wondering what kind of trouble you'd found to get yourself into and if that boyfriend you professed to have was taking good care of you."

"You didn't seem happy to hear from me," she interrupted skeptically, recalling his less than enthusiastic agreement to see her.

John drew a terse breath. "I was trying to forget you. I wasn't used to having a woman haunt me. And you'd made it very clear in New Orleans you preferred to be rid of me. Then you proposed this marriage. My pride took a beating but I agreed. I wanted you so badly, I was willing to do anything to get you." A self-derisive smile played at the corners of his mouth. "I thought once we were together, once I had you in my bed, my preoccupation with you would fade. But it didn't. I cared even more, and it became very important to me for you to honestly care for me. I paid Adelle off because I need you to stay with me because you want to be with me, not because you're afraid of losing the children."

She wanted to believe him. "But you admitted wanting other women," she said shakily.

He frowned at her in confusion. "I never said anything of the sort."

"The night at the fort when Denise almost seduced you, you said it was nice to know your resistance was appreciated," she reminded him curtly.

"That was my ego talking. You were so cool when you asked me if I was going to call her. If the situation had been reversed and one of the male guests had made a pass like that at you, he would have been lucky to walk away from the fort alive." Reaching out, he traced the line of her jaw with the tips of his fingers. "The truth is that resisting her or any other woman hasn't been any effort since you came into my life."

"It was killing me inside to watch her fawn over you," she confessed. "I've been so afraid you were growing bored with me."

"The one thing life with you has not been is boring," he assured her, moving close again and kissing her lightly on the nose.

She wanted to accept everything he was saying without question, but she had been through too much. All of her doubts had to be answered before she could give in to him this time. "If you really care for me, why has it seemed like such a struggle for you to become part of our lives? And—" her voice caught for a moment, but she forced herself to continue ''—why didn't you choose for us to have children?''

A shadow passed over his eyes. ''I wanted very much to be a part of your lives, but I have a deep-rooted fear of rejection. Trying to be open and guarded at the same time isn't easy. And I never knew how you really felt about me. There were times when you lay so gently in my arms, I was certain you honestly cared for me. But then there were others when you were so cool, so controlled.''

''I was afraid of being hurt,'' she admitted.

His voice grew husky with tenderness. ''As for having a child—I want one with you more than I've ever wanted anything. But I couldn't bind you to me that way. I needed you to stay with me of your own free will. It was the night of the murder that I finally decided I had to act. You looked so... haunted when Adelle referred to us as prisoners. I couldn't wait five years to find out if you honestly cared for me.''

She touched his face gently as if afraid this was all an illusion and he might vanish at any moment. "I do care for you very much."

His arms circled her and he drew her tightly against him. "I've been so afraid I would lose you."

"And I've been so afraid you wanted to lose me," she choked out as tears of joy trickled down her cheeks. "I love you so much."

A smile that warmed her very soul spread across his face. "In that case," he said, picking her up in his arms and carrying her toward the house, "would you be interested in getting to work on adding a new member to our family?"

"Very," she assured him.